Forget Me Not

ELLIE TERRY

FEIWEL AND FRIENDS
NEW YORK

A Feiwel and Friends Book
An imprint of Macmillan Publishing Group, LLC

Forget Me Not. Copyright © 2017 by Ellie Terry. All rights reserved.
Printed in the United States of America by LSC Communications US,
LLC (Lakeside Classic), Harrisonburg, Virginia. For information, address
Feiwel and Friends, 175 Fifth Avenue, New York, N.Y. 10010.

Our books may be purchased in bulk for promotional, educational, or business use.
Please contact your local bookseller or the Macmillan Corporate and Premium
Sales Department at (800) 221-7945 ext. 5442 or by e-mail at
MacmillanSpecialMarkets@macmillan.com.

Library of Congress Cataloging-in-Publication Data is available.

ISBN 978-1-250-09627-2 (hardcover) / ISBN 978-1-250-09628-9 (ebook)

Book design by Anna Booth
Feiwel and Friends logo designed by Filomena Tuosto
First Edition—2017

10 9 8 7 6 5 4 3 2 1

mackids.com

for Breya—
who is prettier than a poppy,
brighter than a harvest moon,
and sweeter than a sun-kissed pear
on a late-summer's afternoon

PART ONE

*

AUTUMN

Saturday Morning

I open my dresser drawers,
find them

empty
empty
empty.

What the heck? Not again.
I check the closet, the hamper,
under my *bed*.
"Mom?" I yell so she can hear.
"What did you do with my clothes?"

She doesn't answer me,
which means,

we're moving.

Kitchen Rags

I find her in the living room—
eyes half-closed,
lips pinched tight.
She dumps an armful of socks
into a brown moving box.

"It's over," she says.
"Let's go," she says.
"Don't forget the kitchen rags," she says.

I let out a long sigh.
I won't even get to say good-bye
to my teachers.
I sneak into the bathroom,
close the door so she can't see
me pulling out my hair.

My Hair

My hair is the only thing
I've ever liked about myself.
It's long and wavy and golden.
Dad used to call it
"amber waves of grain"
like in that song,
"America the Beautiful."

Which is why I wish
I didn't wind
strands of it around my finger—

      twirl them once
      twirl them twice

yank them out.
Ouch.

I flush the hair down the toilet.
Can't let Mom see.
Mom said
the next time she sees,
she's going to
cut it.

Fastball

Coach Todd (my private pitching coach) holds a baseball between his fingers as though he's showing me something breakable. "Fastballs are the most important pitches to learn," he says.

Aw, man. I was hoping we could work on my curveball this morning.

"If you can learn to throw them hard," he continues, "you'll be a step ahead of your competition by the time spring rolls around."

Spring. That means I've got five months until Little League tryouts. Five months to learn to throw faster. Harder.

My buddies—Duncan Gray and Nyle Jacques—have done club ball with me for the past four years. Now we're ready to move on to bigger things. Like getting drafted to play on the Royals. Those guys are seriously good. The best of the best. Most of them are expected to make the All-Star team next year.

It would be awesome if Duncan, Nyle, and I could *all* make the Royals. Problem is, there's three of us, and only one open position (and rumor has it, it's pitcher).

Don't Look Back

It would be nice
to stay in one place
long enough to make a best friend,
to *keep* a best friend.

But

every time Mom breaks up
with one of her silly boyfriends,
it's

> grab the keys
> pack the car
> hit the road
> don't look back.

So here we are
driving,
again,
to who knows where,
maybe just away,
tires dizzying themselves
as they speed across the pavement

like all the times before,
the white dashes blurring together into

one
long
line.

We won't slow down until Mom's grip
loosens
and her smile returns.
Then we'll pull over,
make a new home
in whichever town we're in.

Breakfast

Mom tosses me
a bag of cheese puffs.
"Eat."

I scowl,
toss the bag
back.

Nothing,
not even cheese-covered puffs of yum,
can fill the gaping hole
inside my heart—

the gaping hole
where a friend should go.

This Is the Place

We roll to a stop
in St. George, Utah:

bright blue skies,
hills the color of rust
speckled by sagebrush

unlike any town I've seen,
looks like someone took a *paint* brush,
dipped it in a sunset

wish that pretty paintbrush
could sweep away this feeling
of hot air suffocating me.

New Neighbor

I'm sitting by the living room window when a small yellow car pulls into the parking lot of our boring apartment complex. A girl climbs out of the passenger's side, wearing cutoff jeans and a faded blue T-shirt that reads *Gimme Some Space* in large black letters. The afternoon sunlight bounces off her hair like a pot of sparkling gold. Wow. The only girl I've seen with hair that long is Beatriz Lopez. (And hers looks nothing like a pot of gold.)

The girl and the woman with her—I'm guessing her mother—carry boxes of stuff up the stairs. On their second trip up, the girl spots me through the window and smiles, making me forget what I was doing by the window in the first place.

Unpacking My Stuff

Hang up my clothes.
Blow up my *bed*.
Pull out my rocks.
Stack my astronomy books
in a corner.
Done in seven minutes.

The Usual

Mom's sniffling in her bedroom,
so I walk in,
wrap my arms around her waist,
let her tears fall onto my face,
listen to her promise
that someday she'll meet
someone who's

      handsome

and   funny
and   kind
and   most of all

      financially stable,

because
two incomes
is double just
one.

Towels

Mom wipes her eyes.
"Let's finish unpacking,
then we'll go get dinner."

I open a box of bath towels,
groan. Oh no . . .
I left the shampoo bottle
open,
packed it upside down.

The towels are soaked,
but on the bright side,
they smell like sun-kissed pears.

Mom presses her hands
to her temples.
"How about *I* go get dinner
and a new bottle of shampoo,
while *you* wash the towels?"

I nod,
tell her I'm sorry.

She kisses my forehead.
"Love you, Sweet Pea."

After Dinner

The new girl trudges down the stairs with a basket of towels in her arms. (I happen to be sitting by the window. Again.) She makes her way over to the laundry house that all of the residents here share.

I should probably go down and meet her. After all, one of my duties as Black Ridge student body president is to assist in welcoming new students.

I run to my room, sliding down the hall in my socks, and grab some dirty clothes off the floor. "I'm going to do some laundry!" I yell, before heading out the front door. My younger brother, Chonglin, follows me, but I reach the laundry house way before he does and lock him out.

Jerseys

A boy lifts the lid
on a washing machine,
keeps glancing at me
while he puts in his clothes—
mostly baseball jerseys,
like the one he's wearing now,
like the one Dad wore
on Saturday mornings before
everything changed.

Number Fourteen

"I'm Calli," I tell him.
"I moved into number fourteen."

The boy slams the lid,
      presses start,
smiles at me with eyes
the color of cinnamon.

Pears

Calli looks about my age. And she smells like pears, my favorite fruit. I take a huge breath. Ahhh.

"Next door lives Jinsong," I tell her. Crud. "I mean, I'm Jinsong. I live in fifteen. So, what grade are you?"

"Seventh. You?"

"Same."

She lifts herself onto one of the washing machines. Her hair is so long, she's sitting on it. She fans her face with a hand. "Is it always hotter than a volcano here?"

I laugh. "It's cooled down some. You should've been here in the summer. It got up to one hundred thirteen this year."

She shakes her head. "That's awful."

"You'll get used to it."

"Yeah." She smiles. "Maybe I will."

Calli keeps winking and doing this thing with her lips where she pulls them together. It looks like she's going to kiss someone. And she does it so often that I can't help thinking, she must like me or something. (Sweet.)

Tourette Syndrome

By the time I was four,
Mom could tell I had a lot of
"quirks,"
her word, not mine.

I'd chew my nails to bloody stumps,
eat my food in a certain order, and
worry
worry
worry
about everything.

Sometime during second grade,
I started having tics—

      twitching my nose
      tensing my arms
      humming quietly

nothing too bad
nothing anyone paid attention to.
Now my Tourette's
is harder to hide,

but I have to try
if I want to make friends.

I have to try.

Watching TV on Sunday

I don't realize I'm doing it,
twirling and yanking,
until Mom reaches for the craft scissors.
"Okay, Sweet Pea.
Time to fix this little problem, huh?"
She pats the cardboard box in front of her.

No! Please.
Cut off my arm,
but not my hair!

I stare at the screen,
pretend I didn't hear her,
but she's standing there, waiting,
and I don't want to make her upset,
because maybe she'll cry
and she's done enough crying
already.

I drag myself over, slump onto the box,
hold
still
still
still

while she cuts, hacks, chops,
my precious amber waves of grain

short

as short as my new neighbor,
Jinsong's. He
is a boy.

I
am
not
a
boy.

I like wearing skirts.
I like flowers and lace.
And I have two blossoming buds.

Sort of.

Gone

I fight back tears as I stand,
see thousands and thousands of wavy strands
spilled at my feet
like pools of golden blood.

Mornings

Mom says the new haircut
will stop me from
> ratting
> knotting
> pulling out my hair.

She also thinks it'll be quicker,
easier to fix in the mornings,
that I can just run a comb through
while she toasts the bread.

I think it makes
my bald spot more noticeable,
since I can't hide it under my bangs,
but I don't tell Mom this,
she needs more time in the mornings.
No matter how early she sets her alarm,
she's always running late.

Monday Morning at School

I burst through the doors and head straight for the commons, where everyone hangs out until the first bell rings.

A group of girls yell my name, and then giggle to themselves as soon as I look over. (Girls are so weird.)

After stopping to give high fives to some other guys, I finally reach *my* group.

"Hey, Jin!" Duncan says as he and I clasp hands and bump shoulders.

I turn around and give knuckles to Nyle.

"Jinsong," he says, "what's up, bro?"

I shrug. "Not much." I want to tell them about my new neighbor, Calli, but I don't know if she's starting school today or not. I hope she is.

Black Ridge Intermediate School

I stand on the curb
of my tenth new school
wearing a vintage floral shirtdress
with a sailor-style collar and bright red trim.
It's hideous.
But it'll help hide my tics.

Mom rolls down the window
of our Volkswagen Beetle,
aka the Bug.
"Oh, and don't tell anyone about—"

"My Tourette's?
Yeah, Mom. I know.
Bye."

She blows me a kiss and I pretend
to catch it,
put it on my cheek
like always.

I creep toward the big double doors,
breathing in for a count of five,
then letting it out for a count of five.

Mom has to get to her new job at
Rosamelia's Flower Shop,
  she's already late,
so I take the necessary papers
to register myself in the office.
A woman whose badge reads

  MRS. RIVERS

sets down her Diet Coke.
With a broad grin,
she hands me my schedule
and a small pink slip:

  Student: Calliope Snow
  Grade: 7
  Homeroom: D. Kahn, 203

Snow

Snow.

      Snow.

            Snow.

                  Snow.

Snow took
my daddy away,
now it mocks me every time
someone says
my name.

Before Going into 203

I dig in my bag for my lucky pen,
so I can change my last name
on the slip.

I scribble hard.
The ink won't flow.

I fish around for a pencil instead,
but D. Kahn sees me through the glass,
motions for me to come in.

I push through the door,
stand before
an entire class of strangers.

And then,
my tics show up.

My Tics

Wiggle	my nose
pucker	my lips
roll	my eyes
clear	my throat
clap	my hands
tap	my feet.

So much for keeping them hid.

What in the What?

When Calli stumbles into Mr. Kahn's classroom during first period, I nearly fall out of my chair. What did she do to her hair? When I met her the other day, her hair was so long, she could sit on it. And now—I can see her ears. Which is fine. I don't care. She still looks pretty. She just looks really different. And what in the name of Little League is she wearing? And why is she clapping and tapping like that?

I don't have to wonder what Duncan and Nyle think. I hear them whisper, "Freak Girl." I see the smirks on their faces. And one thing's for sure: I am *not* telling them that I know her.

Calli's eyes wander around the room until they land on me. She smiles. Uh-oh.

I nudge my pencil off my desk. Take a long time picking it up. Send a silent wish to the universe (that Calli won't be in any more of my classes).

Welcome

Twenty-seven pairs of eyes stare,
hopefully at my dress,
not at my hair.

D. Kahn extends his hand.
"Hi-de-ho, whom do we have here?"

I give him the slip,
hoping he won't look at it.
"Calli June," I lie.

He winks.
"Welcome to Black Ridge."

Last Names

Truth is,
June's not my last name.
Last names come from fathers

and mine,
is gone.

He left when I was only three,
left Mom and me to be
on our own.

A Day in June

I don't remember much about Dad

but I know we played,
        played in the yard
just him and me
on a warm summer's day

and I know we ran,
        ran through the sprinklers
again and again,
laughing until
we were soaked to the bone

and we shared an orange Popsicle
        out on the deck,
the juice dripping cold
down our chins and our necks

and he caught me a toad,
        a most handsome toad,
set it on my dress so I could hold it,
then he combed his fingers
through my hair
and told me that he loved me.

Introduction

D. Kahn wants me
to tell the class about myself.
I knew he would.
Teachers always do.
And I hate it more each time.

"I—um, I just moved here
from Salt Lake City."

My voice is barely above a whisper,
but I can't help it.
I wish this ugly carpet would

swallow
me
whole.

The Middle

D. Kahn glances
at the pink slip.

No!

"Class, this is Cal-lee-OPE Snow."
He looks at me, winks.
"Did I say it right?"

I shake my head,
feel my face turn red.
Didn't he listen when I told him my name?
"It's just Calli," I say, then add in quick—
"June. Not Snow. June."

"June," D. Kahn murmurs.
"Well, that's in the middle,
we'll have to shift desks."

Almost everyone stands,
groaning as they carry their things
to their new alphabetical place.
D. Kahn reminds everyone
to save a spot for "Beatriz,"

whoever she is,
because she's absent today.

I wish I could take the chair in the back
next to my neighbor,
Jinsong,
or the broken one in the corner.
I'd be happy to hide away
like a turtle inside its shell,
but D. Kahn points to the now empty seat
in the middle.

Garbage Cans

Calli tiptoes into the cafeteria and sits at the empty table next to the garbage cans. Guess she doesn't know there's a reason no one sits there. Who wants to sniff piles of putrid meatloaf while they eat? I wish she didn't have to sit alone. But it's not like she can sit at my table with Duncan and Nyle. No way.

I spot some girls I know in the lunch line and get an idea. I slide my chair from the table. "I'll be right back," I say. "I'm gonna go throw away my food." Duncan and Nyle stare at me like I've lost it. (And maybe I have.)

I make my way over to the garbage cans and slowly scrape the food off my tray, even though I haven't eaten any of it.

"Psst. Psst."

Calli looks over her shoulder at me. "Oh, hey, Jinsong!" she says too loud.

I sweep my eyes across the cafeteria to make sure no one's looking. "Hey"—I talk quickly—"you should move. Away from the garbage cans. They're . . . infected."

"Infected?"

"Yeah, with, um, hand, foot, and mouth disease."

Calli makes a disgusted face. "Ew. Really?"

I sweep my eyes around the room again. "Yeah. Really. You should move over to *that* table." I nod to the one Ivy Andrews sits at. If Calli makes friends with the popular girls, maybe

Duncan and Nyle won't think she's so weird. And I won't have to pretend that I don't know her.

Calli picks up her tray. "Okay! Thanks for the tip!"

"Yep." I rush back to Duncan and Nyle. I don't think anyone saw.

Surrounded

I wish they hadn't
sat by me, this
        giggling
        group of
        girls

whose hair
        and teeth
        and bags
        and clothes
are all exactly the same.

They even have matching
necklaces, twinkling beneath the
        bright
        white
        lights
of the cafeteria.

They seem nice,
telling me their names—
        Ivy
        Hazel
        Gwyneth

but then the
interrogation
begins.

Frog

Ivy wants to know why I'm wearing
"a dress from 1910."

I pretend I don't hear her,
shove a spoonful of applesauce
into my mouth,
instead of explaining:

> I'm hoping this dress
> distracts from my tics
>
> and by the way,
> it's 1940s.

The girl named Hazel
sets down her milk.
"We heard you making a weird noise
this morning. It sounded like a frog."

Oh no,
please don't ask me
about—
Crooooaaaak. Crooooaaaak.
        Ugh!

Every time I think about it,
I do it.

Gwyneth points at me,
"It *was* you making that noise!"
The girls laugh.
They think I'm being funny.

I guess
        the dress
                has failed.

I want to cry,
but swallow the feeling down
with another bite of applesauce.
Tomorrow I'll sit by the garbage cans.

Sometimes

Sometimes my tics
are like gentle whispers,
asking me to do things,
      to say things.
If I try real hard,
I can hold them off
      for a while.

But other times they're like a

SHOUT!

Jumping out so loud and strong
I could never hope to
stop them.

Life-Size

Lucky for me,
my fifth-period art teacher,
Mrs. Ainsley,
doesn't make me introduce myself.
She spends most of the time explaining
how she wants us to paint a self-portrait—
but not just any old head and shoulders,
she wants us to paint ourselves,
"Life-size, head to toe,
as YOU see yourself."

She opens a metal cabinet,
pulls out a nearly completed self-portrait
of a girl named Beatriz,
the same Beatriz
who happens to be absent today.

Mrs. Ainsley carries it
around the room,
showing each one of us.
"Isn't she a wonderful artist?
Beatriz brought this from home
and I thought it'd be the perfect project
to try in class."

It isn't due until April 1,
so we have plenty of time to

ponder,
sketch,
paint.

A Second Me

According to her self-portrait,
Beatriz is a lot taller than me,
with dark brown curls cascading down her back.

I think of my own back—
how bare it is now. No hair
to hug my shoulders. Nothing to keep me warm.

I wish I could tell Mrs. Ainsley
right now: I do NOT want
to do this project. There is already one of me.

Why would I want
a second me? A quiet
girl with too-short hair and a cringing face?

Freak

After school, Duncan and I ride our bikes over to Nyle's. He lives next door to a baseball diamond, so we're always going over there to practice.

I'm winding up my fastball when Duncan starts talking about Calli. "Have you ever seen someone jerk around like that?"

Nyle laughs. "Or wear clothes like that? Dude, that girl's a freak."

They look at me.

I freeze.

"Dude, did you see her?" Duncan asks.

"Yeah." I gulp. "What a freak. Did you see her trip in homeroom?"

They snicker.

I pound the ball into my mitt. My stomach feels sick, like I drank a gigantic glass of rotten milk. I wind up my fastball, again. This time, I hurl it toward Duncan as hard as I can.

Walking

I wish I didn't have to walk home
down this busy street

alone.

There's a million bad things
that could happen to a kid

who's walking home
from school

alone.

Sometimes their faces are on the news,
beneath the phrase:

HAVE YOU SEEN ME?

Number Ten

I pass an orthodontist's office,
spot some red sandstone
surrounding the walkway.

I pick one up,
drop it in my bag.

I'll add it to my collection
in place number ten,
when I get home.

Rocks

I don't have a lot of things,
but I do have a collection of rocks—
kept inside an old egg carton,

ONE DOZEN FARM-FRESH EGGS

printed across the top,
each rock nestled in a bed of white cotton,
solid reminders
of places I've lived.

Each time I add a new one,
I hope it will be the last.

A Chinese Proverb

As I'm sitting in Nyle's kitchen, watching him and Duncan have a competition to see who can fit the most Cheerios on their armpit hair, I remember a proverb my grandfather used to say: *A man should choose a friend who is better than himself.*

Rosamelia's

Instead of going to the new apartment,
I walk seven extra blocks to
Rosamelia's,
where Mom works.

The smell of delicate petals,
the same scent she carries home each night,
wafts through the air,
tickling my nose long before
I reach the shop.

I open the door with my
       right hand,
then touch it with my left
       to make it even.

Mom's busy arranging a wedding bouquet,
barely looks up when I walk in.

"Hi, Mom."
I set my bag on a chair.

"Oh, Sweet Pea," she says,

"can you move that?
I really need the space."

I swing my bag
back to my shoulder,
drum my fingers on the counter.

That's Nice

"How was your first day?" Mom asks.
She's trimming leaves from a dozen long-stemmed
white roses.

"You mean my tenth first day? It was okay.
The building is nice. And I—"

"Oh!" Mom cuts me off.
"I have to tell you about this guy
who came into the shop today. . . ."

My bag slides off my shoulder,
crashes to the floor.
I feel it—
the hope of staying in one place
flutter right out of my heart.
Leave it to Mom to find a new guy
on her first day of work.
She'd better not have his number.

The bell on the front door dings
and a large group of women wearing red feathered
hats and purple dresses
walks in.

Mom greets them,
sets down her scissors before rushing
to the front,

leaving me alone.

Red Flower

I sit on a chair—
the one Mom told me not
to set my bag on.

I study the roses she was trimming,
perfectly uniform in

      size
      shape
      color.

Even the vase they're in is the color of
sn—no—
I'm not going to say it.

I spy a single flower
across the room,
red with a black center,
lying on its side,
tangled up in ribbon and twine.
It isn't hard to see it's been

forgotten.

The edges are curled
and its petals
fold over themselves.

I walk over to the flower,
gently lift it,
place it in the *paper*-white vase
among the dazzling roses.

"There," I whisper.
"There is a home for you.
Now, drink."

These Are Roses

Mom returns to the back of the shop.
When she sees the vase,
her breath catches.
"Oh . . . no, no, no."
She plucks the red flower,
tosses it into a bucket beneath the counter.
"Calliope, did you do this?"

I find my voice. "Yeah."

"That's a poppy," she says.

"It was dying," I say.

We stare at each other.

"Okay, but these"—
she swirls her hands over the vase—
"are roses."

I blink. "Yeah . . . ?"

"Well, poppies don't belong with roses."

"Oh." I frown. "Sorry."

Ginger Ale

As soon as I walk through the door, my mother sends me off to buy more ginger ale. Ever since she found out she's pregnant, she has to have it at all times. She says it takes away her morning sickness. It's so silly she calls it that—morning sickness—because, oh man, it lasts all day.

I ride my bike a few blocks to Nolan's Supermarket, go inside, and head straight for the beverage aisle. I round the corner near the banana stand and crash into Beatriz Lopez. The packets she's carrying fly from her arms and skid across the floor.

"Thanks a lot," Beatriz mutters.

"Sorry," I say, wondering if I should stay to help her or leave before someone from school sees us.

"How's your mom feeling?" she asks. (I guess I'm staying.)

"Not so good." I bend over to help Beatriz collect the scattered packets. When I see that they're powdered *horchata* mixes, I grin.

Our fathers were roommates in college, so I've known Beatriz since the day I was born. We used to play together. A lot. One time her mother took us to the bounce houses for almost four hours. Afterward, we made *horchata*, a drink that tastes like the milk in your cereal bowl after you've eaten Cinnamon Toast Crunch. We used a powdered mix from the cupboard, because we didn't want to wait for Beatriz's mother to make some from scratch. It was the funnest day ever. But now, besides student council meetings or the occasional Lopez-P'eng get-together, Beatriz and I don't hang out anymore. Sometimes I miss those *horchata* days.

Updating My Rock Collection

1. Granite from My Backyard
   (Spokane, Washington)
2. Greenish-Blue Thing I Found in the Street
   (Ritzville, Washington)
3. Cobblestone from an Old Riverbed
   (Walla Walla, Washington)
4. Basalt I Found on a Hike
   (Baker City, Oregon)
5. Piece of Pumice from My Teacher
   (Bend, Oregon)
6. Pebble from the Playground
   (Boise, Idaho)
7. Limestone from the Park
   (Pocatello, Idaho)
8. Lava Rock from Neighbor's Yard
   (Logan, Utah)
9. Salt Crystal from the Great Salt Lake
   (Salt Lake City, Utah)
10. *Red Sandstone from an Ortho's Office*
    (St. George, Utah)
11.
12.

Teeth

I wake in the night
to a pounding heart—
da-dum

       da-DUM

             DA-DUM!
—feel the fear
lying beside me.

I shake my head to clear my brain.
Was I dreaming?
Yes. I was dreaming.
I was a red poppy

     growing
     growing

in a field of white roses.
I was admiring their beauty,
their sameness,
when pointed teeth emerged
from their perfect white mouths

     gnashing
     gnashing

at me
the poppy.

Page Twenty-Seven

It's morning.
We're running late as usual,
no time for hair or toast.

Mom starts the engine.

"Oh no, I forgot something!"
I run back into the apartment,
find my heaviest astronomy book,
open up to page twenty-seven,
carefully lift it out—

the poppy.

Yesterday,
when Mom wasn't looking,
I rescued it from the Bucket of Doom.

I find some clear packing tape in the kitchen,
sandwich the poppy between two layers,
then slip it into the front pocket
of my plaid jumper dress.

The Language of Flowers

In Victorian times,
flowers had meanings
and people gave away certain ones
to communicate.

Forget-me-nots meant
        please remember
        me forever.

Pink carnations meant
        thank you
        so much.

As Mom pulls up
to Black Ridge Intermediate School,
I hope and wish
with every part of my heart,
that in Victorian times,
poppies meant
        courage.

Talk

I walk into the boys' locker room and all I hear is:

"The new girl wears old clothes."

"The new girl rolls her eyes."

"The new girl makes creepy sounds in her throat."

It's all true. But somehow it feels wrong to hear them say it.

Later, in the hallway, I see a bunch of kids standing by the drinking fountain. Calli's third in line, but she never gets any closer, because kids keep cutting in front of her. It reminds me of first grade when this kid on the playground turned to me and said, "Your eyes look different." And I told him it was because I'm Chinese, but he still wouldn't let me go down the slide.

Every Time

Every time I see Jinsong,
he's staring at me—

> in D. Kahn's class
> by the lockers
> on the stairs.

Maybe I'll ask him
to walk home with me today.
He has to go the same way,
anyway.

Stretching in P.E.

I reach for my hair
but find only air,
reminding me
of what Mom did.

Can't twirl.
Can't yank.
Too short.
So, I pick—

pick one lone hair,
one inch-long hair,
pinched between my
fingernails.

But my hands don't feel right.

I need to twirl.
I need to twirl.

"Gah!" I yell,
then cup my hands
across my mouth.

Worse

I tried taking medication
once—
          last year,
          for several months.
All it did was make me sleepy
and make me worry,
which made my tics

worse.

Mom says we can't
afford it, anyway.

Student Council

I can't get away from it. Not even in the student council meeting during lunch.

When the vice president, James McKinley, mentions that Calli's frog croaking made him bomb his math quiz, the secretary, Beatriz (who won only because she threatened half the student body), sits up straight and starts taking notes. "How did I miss this? What's her name, again?" A mischievous grin sneaks across her face.

Oh, great. I see where this is going. I should have known she'd be excited about Calli. Ever since her mother left, Beatriz has been known as the Wicked Comedian of Black Ridge. Everyone thinks she's funny, but no one wants to be friends with her. It's no wonder she eats lunch in Mrs. Ainsley's room most of the time.

"Uh, Beatriz?" I whisper after the meeting's over. "I know your favorite thing in the whole wide world is making wisecracks about other students, but, uh, if I were you, I'd pick on someone besides the new girl, because she knows karate."

Beatriz throws her head back and laughs. "Right." She turns on her heel and stomps out the door to do what she does best. (Hint: It isn't welcoming new students.)

Library Time

I run my fingers
along book spines
as I search for the perfect read.

A voice right behind me says,
"You know that Cantaloupe girl,
or whatever her name is?"

My finger halts on a biography
of Neil A. Armstrong.

      A second voice asks,
      "You mean the new girl?"

I tilt
my head
to listen.

"Yeah, isn't she . . . weird?"

      "I think she's nice.
      But she does roll her eyes a lot."

"I know! She's such a goon.
Cantaloupe June
is a goon!"

Look It Up

I don't dare turn around.
Instead,
I round the corner,
peering over a row of books
to see the two girls.

One is blond with glasses.
I don't know who she is.
But I recognize the other girl,

       Beatriz,

from her self-portrait,
although her face looks a lot sadder
in real life.

The girl with glasses laughs,
taps Beatriz.
"What's a goon, anyway?"

Beatriz feigns a gasp.
"You don't know?
Well, if you don't know,
maybe YOU should look it up."

When Beatriz says *you*
she glances,
over the books,
at me—

Cantaloupe.

Dictionary

I find the dictionary,
flip it open quicker
than Mom flips boyfriends.

G-g-g . . .
g-o
goo, goo—
goon!

>   *1. a stupid person.*

My throat tightens.
My chin trembles.

"I am not," I whisper to
no one.

A Question

After the final bell,
I see Jinsong by the flagpole,
students surrounding him
like a swarm of flies at a picnic.

I scrunch my nose
        jerk my head
                pucker my lips.

Stop it, tics.
I waltz over to the group,
raise my voice so he can hear me.
"Hey, Jinsong?"

Most of the kids turn around,
including Jinsong,
smiling with his cinnamon-colored eyes.

"You want to walk home
together?" I ask.
"I don't like to walk alone."

An Answer

Duncan and Nyle erupt into laughter. They hold their guts. They slap their thighs.

"Ooh, she doesn't like to walk alone," Duncan says in a baby voice, then punches me on the arm. (I'd like to punch the orange hair right off his skull.)

I shift my eyes away from Calli. There's no way I can walk home with her. I'll be teased until I'm eighty-five. "Um . . . uh." I rub my sore arm.

"Dude, Jin," Nyle says, helping me out. "Don't you have to stay after school for that . . . thing, um, with the—"

I snap my fingers. "Yeah! I do. I have a . . . thing." I look at Calli and shrug. "Sorry."

Her mouth falls open and her eyes get all wet-looking. "Oh. No biggie." She slinks away.

A line from the student council agreement I signed at the beginning of the school year pops into my head: *I promise to be a friend to everyone.* The sour-milk feeling creeps into my stomach again.

I sit on the bench by the flagpole and wait for Duncan and Nyle to shut up and go home already. I'm not even listening to what they're saying.

One by one, the buses pull away from the curb, and still, Duncan and Nyle won't stop talking. I tap my sneakers and fiddle with the straps on my backpack. Dang it! Why aren't they leaving?

After every last student, I swear, has gone, Duncan and Nyle finally make their way over to the bike racks. I watch them pedal until they look like two black beetles, crawling in the street.

And then I run to catch up with her.

Unaware

Groups of kids
pass me by,
their backpacks
bouncing
off their butts
as they hurry
to get someplace.

Birds, bikes,
even the early
October air
breezes by,
unaware of me,
unaware of the girl
who has no place
to hurry off to,
except an empty
apartment.

Intrusive Thoughts

Autumn leaves—
yellow, red, orange—
fall from a giant oak
like glowing embers.

Several yards ahead of me,
a purple pickup backs out of a driveway,
careens up the street.

Out of nowhere,
a scary scene plays in my mind,
         my intrusive thoughts,
that's what the school psychologist
called them when I was ten.

I watch in horror as they unfold,
even though I know

they
         aren't
                  real:

         the purple pickup backing out
         its bumper slamming into my side

my body flying through the air, like a superhero
only I'm not, because then I'm falling
and superheroes never fall
my body rolling as it meets the pavement
the driver getting out, screaming for help
my body aching
knuckles bleeding. . . .

Nice

"Yoo-hoo."
A hand waves in front of my face.
"Calli?"

I blink, focus my eyes.
"Oh! Jinsong. Hi."

I take a deep breath in, blow it out.
It never happened, I tell myself.
None of it.
I'm okay. I'm safe.
"So, what are you doing here?" I ask.
"I thought you had a *thing*?"

Jinsong shrugs. He's out of breath.
"Yeah, it's over now.
I ran to catch up with you."

"You ran to catch up with me?"
I can't hold back my smile.
"You're a really nice guy, Jinsong."

Yeah, Right

She called me "a really nice guy." But she's got it all wrong. I'm a big, fat, lying sack of potatoes (with a jerk on top).

Mrs. Sumner, a retired school teacher, is on her porch across the street, watering her various potted plants. She waves wildly when she sees me. "Hi, Jin!"

I wave back. "Hi, Mrs. Sumner." She looks at Calli and squints.

"Oh." I point. "This is Calli."

They wave to each other.

I eye the weird dress/shirt thing Calli's wearing. "So, what's the deal with your clothes?"

She keeps her eyes on the sidewalk, careful not to step on any cracks. "They're clothes, silly. Most people wear them, you know."

I chuckle. "Yeah, but nobody wears clothes like that. Not anymore. I mean, they're nice and all," I lie, "but *some* people—other people—at school, for example, might . . . see them? And think they're . . . interesting?" I don't know why these come out as questions.

A huge grin spreads across her lips. "That's sort of the point."

I stop. She has got to be kidding me. "You *want* people to notice your clothes?"

She crosses her arms, but she's still smiling. "Can you keep a secret?"

Of course I can. "Yeah?"

She turns to me with a dead-serious expression. "Sometimes I do . . . funny things. Embarrassing things. So, I figure, if I'm wearing weird clothes, people will notice the clothes instead." She wiggles her eyebrows. "Good idea, huh?"

More like, ridiculous idea. "You could always just wear a bag over your head."

Calli laughs. And the sound of it makes my stomach feel normal again.

When we reach the doors to our apartments, I don't want to go inside. Calli's like a two-thousand-piece jigsaw puzzle that I want to put together. There are so many questions I want to ask. But my mother knocks on the window and waves for me to come inside. She probably needs help setting up for tonight.

Tic Tock, Eat the Clock

I start at *one o'clock*
and work my way around
the dinner plate that is my boss.

Eat buttered peas,
one
by
one
until the pile is gone.
Next is bread
thick and dry,
not easy going down.

Cough.
Cough.
Gasp!

Unfortunately,
water isn't until *ten*.

      "Take a drink," Mom says.

"I can't. Not yet."

"Drink!"

"I can't." *Cough, cough.* "Not yet."

Mom reaches
across the counter,
slides my glass toward my chest.

She doesn't understand.
No one understands.

Tom

Mom asks me to pick up my things
and tuck in my shirt,
'cause her new
as-of-this-morning boyfriend, Tom,
is coming over
and they're going out tonight.

I leap from the couch.
"Boyfriend? Already?"

Mom blushes.
"He came into the shop yesterday."

Why? Why can't she stay single
for two seconds?
It's like she doesn't know how to live
unless she's in a relationship.

I croak like a frog,
punch my chest.
"So, you're leaving me alone tonight?"

"Oh, Sweet Pea."
Mom sticks out her lip.

"I thought you'd be happy for me.
Hey, isn't that show you like on tonight?
The one with the, um, conjoined twins?"

I plop back onto the couch.
"YOU like that show, Mom.
That's YOUR show."

Idea

If I can keep
Mom home tonight,
she can't go out with Tom,
which means,
she can't break up with Tom,
and we won't move again,

yet.

Excuses

"There's a storm coming."

    "Beautiful night."

"I need help with homework."

    "When I get back."

"I think I have a fever."

    "I think you're fine."

A tight feeling creeps onto my face
and my tics pop out—

    squeeze my eyes
    stretch my mouth
    contort my face into ugly.

Mom frowns, pats my hand.
"And, please, try not to make those faces
when Tom's here.
You remember what Dr. Flagner said."

Mmmm-hmmm.

Thinking While Hanging Lanterns

Calli better not tell anyone I walked home with her today.

Hey, maybe I can be her friend *after* school, just not *during*?

I wish she'd wear some normal clothes.

Is she doing laundry tonight?

I don't know what it is, but there's something . . . exciting about her.

I Think

It was a Friday night—
      I think
when Mom got the call
that would change our lives.
She dropped the phone on the kitchen tiles,
curled into herself,
cried.

Dad had been gone on one of his trips
to Chicago—
      I think
but was on his way home from the airport
when it happened.

There was snow, lots of it,
falling in clumps—
      I think.
And Dad was tired,
really tired,
so he closed his eyes just for a sec,
never opened them again.

Boyfriend #229

Turns out
Tom is
tall
tall
tall,
a telephone
pole.
He's nice,
I guess.
At least
he opens
the door
for her.
I wonder
how long
he'll last?

Bored

During a rerun
of *The Treacherous Twins*,
there's a knock at the door.
I keep watching,
can't answer when Mom's gone.

When the knock comes again,
so do my intrusive thoughts—

> *me answering the door*
> *a police officer removing his hat*
> *telling me that Mom's been hurt*
> *telling me Tom isn't nice like we thought*
> *riding with the policeman to the hospital*
> *seeing Mom in a light blue gown . . .*

"Um, Calli?"
A familiar voice speaks through the door,
shakes me from my daze.
"Your mother told my mother
you're here."

It's Jinsong!

"She said you're watching some show about babies
who were born all connected and stuff?
Which sounds seriously boring.
Sooo, do you want to come over?
It's Zhōngqiū Jié—the Chinese Moon Festival."

He pauses,
probably waiting for my answer,
but I don't give him one.
I'm too busy rushing to the door,
smoothing my wrinkled tee.

Anything involving the moon
has got to be amazing.

Someone

I open the door and see

Jinsong
cinnamon eyes
cheerful grin
bare feet
a friend.

Number Fifteen

Jinsong's apartment is identical to mine,
yet it's completely different.

His place smells like home-cooked food,
while mine smells like freezer meals.

My place sounds like empty silence.
His is filled with love.

My place is decorated with brown moving boxes,
and his with colorful lanterns,

resting on tables, hanging from ceilings,
all lit up, like this feeling inside.

Beautiful

After introducing Calli to my mother, father, Chonglin, and grandfather (he's on Skype), we grab a plate of mooncakes and head up to the balcony. Calli's wearing normal clothes again (a T-shirt and faded jeans).

We sit side by side and stuff our mouths until our bellies feel like bursting. Nothing beats a mooncake with a crispy crust that melts away in your mouth. We drove all the way to Vegas and back yesterday so we could buy them from our favorite bakery in Chinatown. We don't buy them every year, but when we do . . . oh man, we buy a lot.

Calli punches her chest and turns her head to the side real quick. What was that? Some of the "funny things" she was talking about earlier? She looks really embarrassed. But up here, on my balcony, outlined by the full moon's bluish light, I think she looks beautiful.

"You're beautiful," I whisper. Crud. Did I say that out loud?

She turns toward me, her eyes bulging. "Hmm?"

I look away. Up at the sky. "I mean—the moon. It's beautiful. Isn't it?" I am such a nerd. Now she's gonna think I like her.

And then I realize—so what? I do.

Ball Talk

Jinsong's wearing another baseball jersey,
this time with a hat.
"So, you play ball?" I ask.

> He nods. "Pitcher.
> I'm trying out for Little League
> in the spring."

I sigh. "You know,
my dad used to play baseball."

> His eyes light up.
> "Really? What position?"

"Beats me,
that's just what my mom said.
He started when he was a kid,
got a scholarship and everything."

> "That's awesome!
> How come he doesn't
> play anymore?"

"Ummm . . ."

New Subject

"You want to know something
about the moon?"

Jinsong lifts an eyebrow.
"Yeah."

"Okay, are you ready for this?
It isn't round, it's egg-shaped."
My head jerks to the side.
"It's called an *oblate spheroid*, to be exact.
When we look at the moon,
we're looking at one of its ends."

Jinsong makes a *puh* sound.
"I did *not* know that."

I feel my face tightening.
Oh no. Hold them in, Calli.
I tense my body. "Most people don't."

Surprise

I breathe slowly,
trying to stop my facial tics
from coming.

Jinsong's looking

right
at
me.

Maybe I should leave,
before he—

     squeeze my eyes
     stretch my mouth
     contort my face into ugly

Ugh!
These awful tics just
love to surprise me.

But the most surprising thing of all . . .
is that Jinsong doesn't

turn away,
he keeps on looking

right
at
me

smiling with his
cinnamon eyes.

Fun

I want to pluck
the moon from the sky,
swing it around
in circles.

Is this what it feels like
to have a best friend?

Maybe we'll hang out
every day—

have picnics
tell jokes
share secrets
pass notes
have fun.

A Riddle

For the next few minutes, we don't talk, just listen to my family laughing inside my apartment. Calli's pretty much the smartest girl I know. I want to say something smart, too, but don't know what. Then I remember the one time my parents took me to the big Mid-Autumn Festival celebration in Las Vegas.

"You want to know something about Chinese lanterns?" I ask, grabbing one of the paper lanterns set up on the balcony. "We write riddles on them."

"Sounds fun."

"I'm going to write you a riddle," I say. "You get three clues. If you guess the answer, I'll give you a prize."

Calli scowls. "What if I don't?"

"Then you don't get the prize, duh."

I grab a marker from inside and write the first clue on the lantern. Calli says something, but I'm so nervous I can't make out what it is.

When I'm finished, she takes the lantern from me and reads, "I have short hair." She pauses. "Um. A bunny?"

"Not even close! Here's the second clue. Now, think about it." I write it on the lantern.

She reads, "I am cute." She scrunches her nose. "It has to be a bunny!"

For the love of baseball, seriously? Sweat from my hands seeps through the fragile lantern as I write the last clue. I know she's going to get it. (It's so obvious.) And then . . . I'll give her the prize.

She takes the lantern from me. Is she as nervous as I am? With shaking fingers she reads, "Jinsong likes me."

Third Clue

I hold the lantern
with trembling hands.
Can he tell how nervous I am?

I'm pretty sure he's talking
about a girl,
but I don't want him to know,
I know.

'Cause what if I'm wrong?
And what if the girl
isn't me?
So I say the first thing I see.

"Mooncakes!"

Wrong

I think I guessed
        wrong
because all the color drains
from Jinsong's face
and he's quiet until
I start talking about D. Kahn,
how he wants us to decide our careers.

I'll probably be a florist,
        same as Mom.
I like arranging flowers.

Jinsong says he knows
        one hundred percent
what he's going to be—
a professional baseball player.

Great

Mom's date
went "great."

Which is
great

but

not
so
great.

Now I have to
keep them together

forever.

That Was a Close One

It's probably a good thing Calli didn't guess my riddle. If she knew I liked her, she might tell someone. And then that person might tell someone else. And then the entire school would find out.

What was I thinking?

Trim

Saturday morning,
Mom pulls the craft scissors from a drawer,
says it's time
for my first weekly trim,
even though it hasn't been
a full week since she cut it.

"How's the hair pulling?"
she wants to know.
She checks my crown.
"Don't see any new spots."

Cold blades rest against my skin.
I want to scream,
run,
tell her I don't want short hair,
but all I do is bite my cheek,
bend my neck.

One of these days
I'll speak up.

Still

Monday morning
comes much too soon,
like having a bowl of icy water
dumped onto my head
while I'm dreaming of lovely things,
mostly paper lanterns
and mooncakes.

I'm in first-period language arts,
reading my library book,
when my butt and legs get all twitchy.

I   shift   shift   shift
swing my legs

      in
out
      in
out
      in
out.

Something hits my back.

I turn around.
Beatriz frowns. "Can't you sit still?"

I bet a hundred thousand bucks
if Beatriz felt like something was

     poking her ribs
     tickling her nose
     pinching her legs

she couldn't
sit still, either.

Normal

My eyes squeeze shut
and my mouth opens wide
into a silent scream.

Annoying tics.

I face forward,
glue my eyes to the whiteboard.
Beatriz taps my shoulder.
I turn around again. "What?"

"Do you plan on making those weird
faces all year long?"

I'd like to ask her if she plans
on being a
    beast
all year long.

She continues,
"Because if you ever want to get a
friendship locket,
you might want to act
normal."

She points around the room.
"Ivy, Hazel, Gwyneth, Tilly, Grace.
They all have friendship lockets.
Every girl at Black Ridge has one,
except you."

I glance at Beatriz's neck.
"And you."

Busted

D. Kahn strolls past us,
taps on our desks.

"Reading time
is quiet time, ladies."

Strike One

Every five minutes during reading time, Calli pulls something flat from her pocket, studies it for a while, and then puts it back. What the heck is it? I have to know. So the next time she pulls it out, I ball up a piece of notebook paper and make my way real slow toward the trash can.

I'm so busy looking at her hands that I don't notice her bag lying on the floor.

I trip.

And to keep myself from flying forward (and looking like a total loser) I grab onto Calli's arm. She startles and lets out a small yelp.

Mr. Kahn clears his throat. "Is there a reason you are out of your seat right now, Mr. P'eng?"

"I'm throwing this paper away."

He strokes his beard. "And grabbing other students?"

I shake my head, but Mr. Kahn asks to speak with me after class. Strike one.

I throw away the wadded piece of paper and head back to my seat. Great. Just great. I'm probably on Mr. Kahn's bad side now. All because Calli had to make me curious. And she wasn't even looking at anything cool. She was holding a silly red flower!

Trouble

D. Kahn calls me up to his desk.
I swallow,
let out three long breaths

I'm in trouble
I'm in trouble
I'm in trouble

He Whispers

"Miss June, are you feeling all right?"

      "Yes. I'm fine."

"You seem a bit nervous,
a bit upset."

      It's nice of him to ask,
      but I'm not supposed to tell.
      "I'm okay," I say.

He scratches his beard.
"All righty, then.
Just know I'm here if you need to talk."

      I nod. "Thanks."

After Class

Mr. Kahn gives me the You-Know-Being-the-Student-Body-President-Means-You're-the-Example speech.

"Yes, sir."

"All right." He winks. "No more interruptions after this, okeydokey?"

I give him a thumbs-up and exit the room before he can make me say "artichokie," like he usually does.

Pre-cip-i-ta-tion

In science, Mrs. Locke
says the word

    precipitation.

It's a fun-sounding word, so I
immediately say it in my head

    precipitation.

Next, I have to test
all of the syllables.

    pre-CIP-i-TA-tion.

And then, I just can't stand it.
I *have* to say it out loud.

    "Precipitation!"

Groups

We divide into small groups
to analyze pre-CIP-i-TA-tion graphs
from different cities.

Each time someone in my group says
       pre—that word—
I have to repeat it,
feel each letter on my tongue,
hear the stresses of each syllable
pronounced in

       exactly
       the right
       way.

It doesn't take long for my group,
especially Beatriz Lopez,
to notice.

Copycat

After Beatriz says

    —that word—

a bazillion times,
and I repeat

    —that word—

a bazillion times,
she turns to me and asks,
"Are you sure your name isn't
Copycat?"

Everyone in my group
laughs.
I clench my teeth

hard

so hard, I swear

I feel
them
crack.

He Doesn't Even Look

Soon, echoes of
       —that word—
pop up
all over the classroom.

Mrs. Locke
doesn't do anything to stop it,
and I'm not surprised,
because all she witnesses
is her students discussing their assignment.

But someone

       knows
       sees
       hears

yet

doesn't say a word
doesn't move a muscle
doesn't even look up from his book.

Biting My Tongue

I hear it. I hear it all. And it bothers me—them teasing her like that. It *is* funny, I'll admit, how she repeats it. But they don't have to throw it at her like a baseball pitch to the face.

I stare at my book. Tell myself the teasing will stop. Any second now. But it doesn't. Not for a long, long time.

There's a war going on inside my brain/heart/head/whatever. One side wants to be Jinsong P'eng, Black Ridge student body president (and friend to all). The other wants to be best buddies with Duncan Gray and Nyle Jacques. I think only one can win.

PART TWO

✳

WINTER

Three Months

Mom comes home late
from her date
with Tom,
smelling like flowers
and pizza
and people.

They've been dating for three months now.

She tiptoes into my room, kisses my cheek,
probably thinks that I'm asleep.

      "How'd it go?"

She startles, then grins.
"Sweet Pea. You're awake."

      I bob my head,
      smile a sleepy smile.

"We had fun," she says.
"Played laser tag," she says.
"With some of Tom's friends," she says.

She strokes my eyebrows,
like she did when I was little.

I close my eyes,
pretend I still am.

Chance

Mom glides her hand
across my hair and gasps.
"We forgot
your trim last week!"

My eyes shoot open.
I sit up.
She's right.
She's right!
This
is
good.
Here's my chance.
The perfect opportunity.
I've got to tell her
how I feel.
Now.

I lick my lips,
open my mouth.

A whistling sound
comes from the kitchen.
"Tea's done!"

Mom pats my hand,
leaves my room.

Opportunity splatters
the carpet and walls
like an airborne bowl of
spaghetti.

Next Time

Next time,
I'll tell her.

Even if
it makes
her cry.

Jell-O

November, December, and January aren't much different. Beatriz points out every face Calli makes. She laughs at every sound. (She gets the other kids to join in, too.)

And every day after school, after my "thing" is done, I meet Calli by the old oak tree and we walk the rest of the way home, together. We talk about everything—well, no, that's a lie. We never talk about how I sit in the corner like a blob of Jell-O, listening to it all but saying nothing.

Possible

The thing about
Tourette's
is that it's possible
for new tics
to appear overnight

like the frost on my window
one chilly morning
in February.

Some Amazing Trick

During language arts
the top of my head

itches
tickles
tingles.

My hand forms into a fist,
whacks the spot with my knuckles.

Beatriz whispers from behind,
"Everyone watch Calli."

The spot tingles again. Uh-oh.
I straighten my neck,
my back.
No, head, I tell it.
You do not itch. I do not feel you.

I casually scratch the spot,
but still,
it itches, tickles, tingles.
Maybe if I ignore it long enough,
the feeling will go away?

I
resist
resist

but the feeling gains momentum,
like a bicycle rolling down a hill
until it is out of control.

whack! whack! whack! whack!

Beatriz silently applauds.
A few kids laugh.

Yep, she's a beast.

White

On my way to the cafeteria,
I pass Mrs. Ainsley in the hall,
give her a slight smile
before heading down the stairs.

She calls out my name,
pronounces it wrong.

I stop.

Throngs of hungry seventh-graders
shuffle around me as I wait
for Mrs. Ainsley to reach the middle step.

"I noticed you haven't sketched
your self-portrait yet," she says.
"Your canvas is still
                completely white."

Truth is,
I've sketched my self-portrait
dozens of times,
I just erased it afterward.

"Yeah, I know.
But I've finished five other projects."

She cocks her head.
"True. But I'd like you
to focus on your self-portrait now,
okay?"

Grrrr. "Okay."

Valentine

All of the girls
are asking the boys,
"Will you be my valentine?"
even though
Valentine's Day
isn't until next week.

I want to ask Jinsong,
but I chicken out in homeroom,
because of my head-whacking tic.
And I chicken out in science
because, well,
because I'm a chicken.

But when I see him in the cafeteria,
standing by the salad bar,
scooping heaps of sunflower seeds onto his plate,
I decide it's now or never.

Salad and Sugar Cookies

Calli's walking toward me. She looks pretty today. Is she wearing lip gloss? I do a quick scan of the cafeteria. No one's watching. Good.

"You want to know something about the moon?" she asks. She doesn't wait for my answer. "This astronaut—Stuart Roosa—he took some seeds with him on the Apollo 14 mission, and when he brought them back, they were planted all over. People called them *moon trees*."

"Cool." I head for my table.

"Wait," she says, stepping in front of me, "wanna be my valentine?"

Crud. I was hoping she wouldn't ask. Not because I don't want to give her anything, but because she won't understand why I have to say no—I can't risk everyone thinking I'm a loser. I look down. At my salad. The lettuce looks wilted and sad. I close my eyes. Force the words out. "I already have a valentine. Sorry."

Calli doesn't say anything, just walks backward until she bumps into Duncan.

"Watch where you're going, Pea Brain!" he yells.

What a jerk face. Who does he think he is? Not the winner of the Who-Can-Fit-the-Most-Cheerios-on-His-Armpit-Hair Contest. (That's Nyle.)

My heart feels like it's being pushed through an electric

orange juicer. Calli has to have a valentine, even if it can't be me. I scan the lunch line for someone who can help me out and I spot Kenny Gunn, aka the Nicest Kid in School. Seriously, this kid is so nice he holds doors for teachers.

I walk up to Kenny and explain my offer. He accepts, so I give him my big sugar cookie with pink icing as payment. I don't know if my plan will make Calli happy or not, but I feel better.

Never Mind

I scurry away—
head jerking,
lips puckering,
eyes following the painted lines on the floor—
to my usual place
by the garbage cans.

I sit,
count the blue specks
in the table.

Does Jinsong really have a valentine?
Or does he just
not want to be mine?

Kenny

A short kid with bright blue eyes
and wide-rimmed glasses
joins me at the Garbage Table.
I think I've seen him in my science class before.

"Hi. I'm Kenny," he says.
"Will you be my valentine?"

I glance across the room at Jinsong.
He's looking at me.
He's smiling at me.
What the heck?
Did he have something to do
with this?

I hunch my shoulders,
tilt my head. "Fine with me."

Science Class

Mrs. Locke is at the board
explaining meta-MOR-pho-sis
when my shoulders jerk:

                        forward.

backward.

upward.

I clap my hands,
tap my feet:
tip-tap, *tip-tap*,
feel everybody staring at me,
like hungry coyotes
watching a baby jackrabbit.

Even Mrs. Locke
halts her presentation, furrows her brow.
"Is everything okay?"

I slide down in my chair,
keep straight-faced as though
I haven't done anything wrong.

Because I haven't.

Storm

The classroom door swings open
and all eyes shift from me
in unison.
The school librarian,
      Ms. Emerson,
sticks her head in the doorway.

Mrs. Locke sets down her marker,
tells us to read page 109,
before stepping into the hall.

As soon as the door shuts,
my tics start up again.

      forwardbackup
      forwardbackup
      clap-clap
      tip-tap!

Eyes wander in my direction.

Calm down, Calliope!
I squeeze my body

tight
tight
tight

but it's no use,
they just keep coming,
pelting me like hail in a storm
until I'm dented up.

I glance at page 109,
try to read,
but the words blur together
under drops of rain from my eyes.

Poison

I tap my foot, again—
hard,
so hard,
I launch my chair backward,
hit my head
on the desk behind me,
before landing on my back
on the floor.

First, I notice pain.
Second,
laughter,
coming from every corner of the room,
burning my ears
like poison.

Crud

I want to race over. Check Calli's head for bruises. Help her up. Give her a hug. Tell her everything will be okay. Yell at Beatriz. (She was the one who started the laughing.) I want to do all of these things . . . but I don't move. Instead, I pretend to read page 109.

My chair grows hotter by the moment. I'm surprised I haven't jumped out of it yet. Surprised that even though my butt is burning, my body is frozen stiff. I'm burning, yet freezing. Worst feeling ever.

Kenny gets up and sprints across the room toward Calli. What does he think he's doing? I hired him to be her valentine, not her BFF, but hey, I guess I'm glad that he got up. (Because now I don't have to.)

Caring

Kenny rushes to my side.
"Are you okay?"

I look into his bright blue eyes—
the eyes of the only person
on the ground
caring.
I nod as my shoulders jerk
forward, backward, upward.

"What's wrong?" he asks. "Are you cold?"

What am I supposed to tell him?
Tell everyone? I can't just blurt it out—
I have Tourette syndrome!

Can I?

Nothing

My lips part,
ready to speak,
but nothing comes out.

I have to get away,
have to hide what's inside.

I roll to my feet,
locate the door.
With tears spilling over
like a rushing waterfall,

I run.

Running

Past all the kids in the classroom,
past Mrs. Locke in the hall,
past the music room and the cafeteria.

After turning the corner,
I slow down,
crawl into the space beneath a drinking fountain,
let them all out—
my tics and my tears.

Coward

I can't believe it. I just sat there. Calli fell. She was hurt. And I just sat there. Let kiss-up Kenny help her up. I've got to be the worst student body president in the history of student body presidents. Not to mention the most horrible friend ever.

What's the big deal, anyway? Who cares what Duncan and Nyle think of her? Who cares what the whole school thinks of her? All that matters is what I think of her. And I like her. I like her a lot. I like that she smells like pears. I like that she laughs at my jokes. I like that she's different and puzzling and smart and easy to talk to.

But after today—after what I did (and didn't do)—I doubt she'll ever want to see my face again. Or talk to me. Or forgive me.

So, I'll just disappear now. The coward will disappear.

Don't Tell

When I was eight
and Dr. Flagner,
    the neurologist,
said, "It's Tourette's,"
Mom sucked in a breath,
choked on her own spit.
I popped a sucker into my mouth,
happy to have a name
for all the weird things I did.
Dr. Flagner also said
that if he were me,
he wouldn't go around telling everybody,
because Tourette's is a very

misunderstood

disorder
and if people knew,
they'd treat me different,
expect me to curse
spit in their face
give them the finger,
    because that's all they've seen in the movies

even though not everyone
who has Tourette's
does that.

Telling

Kenny races around the corner,
skids to a stop in front of me.
He wants to know
          what's wrong.

I want him to go away.

Mrs. Locke and Ms. Emerson
come around the corner.
They want to know
          what's wrong,
too.

I wipe my nose on my sleeve,
mentally punch myself
for not telling sooner.
I should have told
everyone
my first day here.

"I can't hold them in
anymore," I say.

      "Hold what?" Kenny asks.

I let out a long breath.

"My tics.

My Tourette's."

Feelings

I lie on a table in the nurse's office,
an ice pack pressed
to my head.

Ms. Baumgartner,
the school counselor,
comes in,
says we should "talk"
about "life" and "feelings."

I really don't feel like
"talking" about anything.
Especially "life" and "feelings."

Ms. Baumgartner calls Mom,
puts the phone to my ear.
But I don't listen when she tells me
it'd be a good idea
to talk to Ms. Baumgartner.

She doesn't understand.
No one understands.

The Reason

Mrs. Locke and Kenny return to the classroom, and Mrs. Locke explains that Calli has Tourette syndrome. I don't know what that is, but Mrs. Locke says it's the reason Calli fell back in her chair and we were all wrong to laugh at her.

For the record, I didn't laugh. (I just didn't help her up.)

The air around me is thick. It's choking me. I have Mrs. Locke sign my hall pass and I hightail it to the boys' bathroom, where I splash my face with freezing-cold water again and again.

I'm staying in here until the last bell rings.

Ms. Baumgartner

I lower myself onto a cushioned chair,
confused,
feeling more like a
complicated math problem
    than a girl.

Ms. Baumgartner sits in the chair next to me,
says my name—
wrong.

I frown.

She grins,
asks me if I would like to tell her what happened
that made me so upset.

I would not like to tell her what happened
that made me so upset,
so I just sit there,
stare at the shiny silver strands
in her hair,

resist the urge
to jerk my shoulders
or croak like a frog.

Holding It In

Ms. Baumgartner crosses her legs,
leans closer.
"Mrs. Locke mentioned
you're having some trouble?"

I nod. "My tics."
As soon as I say the word,

they   l   e   a   p

out of me
like grasshoppers in a brush fire.

forwardbackup!
forwardbackup!
clap-clap!
tip-tap!

"I was trying to hold them in," I tell her.

"I see." A deep line forms between her eyes.
"And does holding them in
make them go away?"

"Well, no."

"Calliope."
She says my name right!
"If a person needs to yawn,
   they yawn.
If a person needs to sneeze or cough,
   they do."

Sticky Note

Ms. Baumgartner writes
on the sticky pad in front of her.
I can tell she's close to smiling.
Will she laugh at me, too?

"What you need," she says, "is to . . ."

She hands me the sticky note.
It reads

Let them out!

I shake my head.
"No way.
Nuh-uh.
I can't do that."

I Am Calliope June

Ms. Baumgartner's mouth explodes
into an enormous grin.
She tells me to sit tall—

     head straight
     shoulders square
     feet on the floor.

"Say, 'I am Calliope Snow.' "

     "It's June."

"All right, then say, 'I am Calliope June.' "

     I shift my butt on the chair,
     mumble, "I am Calliope June."

"I am smart."

     "I am smart."

"I am strong."

     "I am strong."

"And I can do ANYTHING . . ."

    I pause.
    "Almost anything . . ."

"I set my mind to do."

    I roll my eyes,
    but not for the reason
    she thinks.

Finally

The bell rings. And thank goodness. Because some kid came into the bathroom a while ago and really stunk up the place.

Calli's last class is down hall A, so I take the stairs by hall D and exit through the back doors.

I hide behind the back of the school until everyone has left. And just to be extra careful, I take the long way home (even though it's snowing)—through the park, behind Nolan's Supermarket, and over someone's backyard wall.

When I reach the last turn, I gaze at the large oak tree in the distance. At the tiny figure of a girl in an old, poufy dress. Waiting in front of it. Waiting for me.

Dang it. Why'd she have to move here? She's ruining my life! All I used to worry about was how hard I could throw my fastball. Now everything's so complicated.

I kick a rock as hard as I can and send it tumbling into the street. I take one last look at Calli before running the rest of the way home. When I get inside, I lock the door behind me.

Waiting

I'm waiting for Jinsong at the big oak tree
even though
I'm blazing mad at him.

He's late.
I don't know why.
All I know is
there's a sore spot on the back of my head
and my chest feels like it's being squeezed—
not in a huggy-lovey sort of way.

Eventually,
I give up,
finish walking home alone.

When I get upstairs, I

                            fling

my bag
across the room,
drape
myself across my *bed*,

watch snowflakes out my window as they

flit

                  float

      fall

to
the
ground,

disappear.

Note on the Fridge

Sweet Pea,

I'm going over to Tom's.
It might be a late night.
Make yourself some dinner &
get your homework done.

Love,
      Mom

P.S. Please unload the dishes.

Groan

The last time Mom said,
"It might be a late night,"
it was.
And we moved the next day.

I'm so tired of watching her smile
turn to tears,
tired of listening to her worries and fears
and sad love songs,
like "How Do I Live."

Can't Mom see . . .
if she'd stop dating,
she'd stop getting hurt,
we'd stop moving,
we'd both be happier?

But she's convinced
she can't make it alone.
*Two incomes
is double just one.*

So this is it?
We'll be leaving in the morning?

Maybe it's for the best—
    Jinsong's acting weird.
    Beatriz won't leave me alone.
    I have no friends.
    I've failed.

Plan

I'll just forget about Calli. Ignore her. Go to Duncan's after school, instead of meeting her at the oak tree. I should never have walked home with her the first time. Just like when you feed a stray dog, it keeps coming back.

Good-Bye

I want to say good-bye to   him,
even though I'm mad at   him.
I've never had a friend like   him.
Oh, how I'm going to miss   him.

The P'engs

I slip on my shoes,
walk over to number fifteen
to see if he's home,

but I get my answer
all too soon.
The blinds are open
in the P'engs' front room.
Jinsong's home all right.

    I blink
and blink
and blink
and blink

can't believe my eyes.

The P'engs are eating dinner,
       a dumpling soup,
     I think,
and sitting right next to Jinsong
is none other than

Beatriz Lopez.

Cold

A cold tingling
starts in my chest,
spreads to the rest
of my body.

Guess
I was wrong
about Jinsong's
riddle.

The answer might
have been a girl,
but it obviously
wasn't me.

I tiptoe back
to number fourteen,
run upstairs
to my room.

Dinner

The Lopezes come over for dinner and my parents make me sit right next to Beatriz, which gets me thinking about Calli. (Even though I told myself I wasn't going to think about her anymore.) Man, I hate this feeling. There's a lump in my throat that won't go down, no matter how many times I swallow.

I wait until our parents have migrated to the living room, and then I turn to Beatriz. "I know what you've been doing, and you need to stop."

She pauses, her cup frozen in midair. "I can't get a drink of water?"

"I'm talking about Calli June," I snap.

Beatriz snorts, refills her cup, and takes a sip. "If you're talking about everyone laughing today, I didn't start it. Duncan did. And why do you care anyway?"

I rub my forehead, thinking of what I can say. She can't know the truth.

"Wait a minute." Beatriz narrows her eyes. "You don't, like, *like* her? Do you?"

I tense my neck and slam my fork on the table.

Beatriz cough-laughs. "Oh my gosh! I can't believe *you* . . . like *Calli*."

"Look," I tell her, "I'm the student body president. So I'm supposed to be friends with everyone. That's all."

Beatriz's teasing smile fades and she sets down her cup.

"Really? And do you think you're doing a good job of that? Being friends with everyone? Because I can't remember the last time you called or texted me to hang out."

I push my chair away from the table and stand. "Well, since your mother left, you're not all that fun to hang out with."

Can't Sleep

Can't stop thinking
about falling over.

Over
and over
and over.

Can't stop
the echoing sounds of laughter.
Can't go to school
ever again.

I wriggle from my blankets,
crawl to the hall,
curl into a ball,
soak up moonbeams as they fall
through the window.

The silver swirls
reach out,
welcoming me,
pulling me toward them
like they do to the
seas.

Poem in My Head

I am Calliope June.
I wish I could fly to the moon.
There'd be no one there
to laugh or to stare
and no one to call me a goon.

Same Routine, Sort of

I get up bright and early,
dress,
eat,
pack my clothes for the road trip I know
is coming.

Mom clears her throat,
shouts from her room.
"What are you doing out there?"

I fold the kitchen rags,
shout right back.
"Didn't you break up with Tom?"

She doesn't answer me,
which means,

it was a false alarm.

Strike Two

The student council comes in early to paint posters for our upcoming fund-raiser. Beatriz is here, since she's the secretary. She's ignoring me, which wouldn't normally seem strange, but after dinner last night, it feels about as normal as getting my blood sucked by leeches.

I'm sure Calli's mad at me for yesterday. Now Beatriz is, too. (I'm pulling double duty here.) Why don't they just hand me a first-place trophy that says *Worst Friend on Earth*?

I'm sitting on the floor, painting blue letters, when I hear, "Hey, Jinsong."

I look to my left. Feel something cold and wet hit my cheek. My eyes follow the familiar sneakers up to Beatriz's smirking face.

"Tag. You're it!" She runs to the other side of the cafeteria, laughing.

I scramble to my feet and chase after her. When I catch up, I put her in a headlock and paint the side of her face a nice shade of wild-berry blue.

"Mr. P'eng!" Mr. Kahn's voice echoes across the cafeteria. I drop my brush. Let go of Beatriz. Strike two.

She limps back to the posters like she's injured. That's Beatriz for you. The secretary who gets away with everything. But for a minute there, I thought I saw a glimpse of the friend I used to know.

February 14

Balloons and bears
Pinks and whites
Cards and candy
Hearts
Pasted on walls
Filling up lockers
Covering desks
Except for mine
But wait till lunch
Kenny will come
Bring me a valentine

He Loves Me . . .

I leave my desk to sharpen my pencil
and when I return I find:
a hot pink mug, filled with gum
and two large valentines.

I pick up the first,
expecting it to be from Kenny, but
hoping,
hoping it might be
from somebody else.

It reads:

> *Will you be my valentine?*
> *You are so pretty. I want to kiss you.*
> *Love, love, love forever,*
> > *Jinsong*

I press my palms to my cheeks.
I knew it.
I knew he liked me.

Not

I unfold the second valentine.

> *What I love about you:*
> *Your hair.*
> *Your clothes.*
> *Your face.*
> *Your nose.*
> *Your froggy croaking.*
> *And most of all . . .*
> *that you are GULLIBLE!!!*

Duncan and Nyle explode into hysterics.
I glare at them,
confused.

Duncan walks past my desk,
grabs the valentines,
smirks.
"Jinsong thinks you're butt-ugly."

Sinking

Bam!
Bam!
Words slam
against my heart,
knocking it from
its place,
sinking it to
my shoes.

Exposed

I grip the edges of my chair,
don't dare look over at Jinsong.
If only I had my hair, I could hide,
hide my face from everyone,
especially him.

But no,
my face is just

                              out there

bare and pink as a newborn rat
for the whole wide world to see.

From Me

I wish Calli knew. Knew how much I like her. Knew that I think Duncan and Nyle are jerks for what they did. Knew why Kenny didn't show up to give her a valentine. (He's at home, puking up his guts.)

After school I ask my mother to drive me to a flower shop, but not Rosamelia's. I don't want Calli to see.

The shop we find is busy, crammed with people of every age and flowers of every color—pink, white, orange, purple, and yellow. But I don't want those. I'm searching for a certain red one.

Five O'Clock

Mom calls to say
she's finished with work,

      but

Tom came by the shop,
wants to take her out to dinner.

Things must be going really well.
So why don't I feel
like jumping up and down?
Why do I want to punch
a hole in the wall?

"Okay," I tell her, "have a good time."

I rummage through the freezer,
find a frozen meal:

      fried chicken
      creamed corn
      mashed potatoes that look like glue

zap it in the microwave.

While I wait,
I do a funny thing with my jaw—
thrust it

        forward
                forward
                        forward.

Uninvited Guest

I take a bite of chicken,
chew,
thrust my jaw forward, again.
This time it

    pops!

sounds like tiny bits of bone
are breaking from my jaw.

Sneaky new tic.
I never know when
one will decide
to knock on the door to my brain
like an uninvited guest:

> *Surprise! I'm here!*
> *I won't stay long.*
> *Or maybe I will.*
> *Which room is mine?*
> *I'm hungry. Feed me.*
> *Where do you keep the towels?*

I finish my chicken before I feel

the urge to do it again.

I won't.
I won't.
I tell myself.

But then, I do.

And it hurts.
And the more it hurts,
the harder I push.
I cry out in pain, cradle my face,
brace myself,
for I know . . .
it is only a matter of moments
before it comes again.

Pudding

My jaw will be sore for a   week.
Can't open my mouth to   speak.
Why am I such a   freak?

It's pudding
and yogurt
and applesauce—

all things soft
for a while.

Armed

Armed with a dozen red flowers called "poppies" and a little card that reads *Happy Valentine's Day!* I sneak up to number fourteen and knock.

Calli doesn't answer.

I knock again.

And again.

Crud. She probably knows it's me. Maybe she'll answer if I go away? I knock hard and fast, then sprint into the parking lot to hide.

Her door creaks open. She takes one look at the flowers and starts to shut the door, but stops. Scoops up the vase. Takes the whole thing inside. Yes! But then—I watch through the window as she feeds the flowers, one by one, to her garbage disposal.

PART THREE

SPRING

Going

Mom's going to a spring florist convention
in Las Vegas,
which is only two hours away,
but she'll be gone for three whole days.

Three
        whole
                days!

"You'll sleep at the P'engs,"
she tells me, "just carry over
your pillow and blanket.
They have a futon for you."

I don't know what a *futon* is, but no.
I am not sleeping over at a boy's house,
especially Jinsong's.
We aren't friends anymore,
but even if we were,
staying overnight at a boy's house is

just
plain
weird.

Friday Night

When Mrs. P'eng comes to the door,
      I lie,
tell her I'm not feeling well,
       tell her
I don't want to spread my germs.

Never Before

I've been at home
alone before,
but

I've never been
overnight
alone before,

never checked the locks before,
one hundred and one times before
going to bed alone before.

I've never heard these sounds before,
creaking
in the dark before,

never been so scared before—
I pile the chairs
by the door before.

Never before.

Passing the Time

The apartment feels empty
Saturday morning,
different.
How does it know?
How does it know Mom's gone
out of town?
And not just up the street at Rosamelia's?

There's nothing on TV,
so I pass the time by flipping through
my astronomy books
and building a space mobile with colored paper.

I'm in the middle of constructing Uranus
when there's a knock at the door.

"Calli, hon, it's Mrs. P'eng."

I smooth my hair,
swing the door open,
find
       Mrs. P'eng,
       her rounded belly,
       and Jinsong.

When I look at him, Jinsong crosses his arms,
checks the bottom of his shoes
       for something.

Mrs. P'eng asks if I'm feeling better,
says they're headed
to the county fair
and wouldn't I like to come?

Ghost

Calli says yes, which surprises me, because I'm pretty sure she hates my stinking guts.

The ride out to the fairgrounds is horrible. Calli talks to my parents and Chonglin, but doesn't say anything to me—doesn't even acknowledge I exist. For all I know, I'm a ghost and she can see right through me.

When my parents mention they're taking Chonglin to see the magic show (for the second time), Calli asks, "Do you mind if I head over to the carnival?"

"That's fine," my mother tells her, "as long as you and Jinsong stay together."

"Okay," Calli says, but the way she winces as we turn to leave makes me think it's not.

And why would it be? Why would she want to hang out with me? My grandfather's proverb says we're supposed to choose friends who are *better* than us. Not ten times worse.

Walking to the Carnival

"You don't have to follow me."

"But, my mother said—"

"Why don't you go find your *real* friends?"

"My *real* friends?"

"Yeah, you know, Duncan, Nyle . . . Beatriz?"

"Calli . . ."

I don't want to hear the rest.
Whatever he says is probably going to hurt.

Dust

I take off running,
toward the rides,
kicking up dust clouds
as I go.

You Win

I run into Duncan, Nyle, and the rest of the gang by an inflatable pitching booth, but I don't see Calli anywhere. Crud. Where'd she go? Either she suddenly had to use the bathroom, or she's trying to ditch me.

Nyle puts an arm around my shoulders when he sees me. "Jin! My man! Come play."

Duncan steps out of the booth and sets the ball in my hands. "Yeah, let's see if you can top my speed!"

"Guys, I—I'm kind of busy right now."

"Oh, come on."

I wind up for the pitch. Everyone's watching. I know I can beat Duncan's score. Nyle's, too. But my arm freezes. I can't concentrate on the target. I have to find Calli, have to tell her I'm sorry for everything.

"Dude, just throw the ball already," Duncan says.

I relax my stance. Toss the ball to the ground. "You win, Duncan. I gotta go."

I find Calli ten minutes later, leaning against a metal fence behind the Ferris wheel. She's making those faces and doing those "funny" things that make her, her. My heart lurches into my throat and my head spins around like a carousel. I have to fix things.

"Calli!"

She looks up. Scowls. Starts walking away. She *was* trying to ditch me. Dang it. This is gonna be harder than I thought.

I jog to catch up with her. "Hey! Come ride the Ferris wheel with me."

Conflicted

I want to punch him and hug him
at the same time.
Oh, how I wish,
we could still be friends.
Maybe I should go with him?
Maybe it'll be okay,
listening to what he has to say?

We Sit

Side by side
in one of the cars.

Silent as
the large wheel turns.

Flying back
into a flaming sunset.

Cotton Candy

"So," Jinsong says.

"So?" I say,
staring at my lap.

"I hear the cotton candy
is really good this year."

I gawk at him.

"We should try some."

I cross my arms,
shake my head.
"You've barely noticed I'm alive
for the past two months,
and now . . .
you want to talk about cotton candy?"

He wrings his hands, shrugs.
"I just don't know where to start."

I Blink

"How about you start with
      why you ignore me at school?
Or why you didn't
      want to be my valentine?
Or how you could be so rude
      and leave flowers at my door?"

Sorry

I bite my lip, grip the metal bar in front of us. "I'm sorry," I say. "I was embarrassed."

She stares at her hands and asks what I wish she wouldn't. "Of me?"

I let my gaze wander far away, to the parked cars that look like toys. "I was too embarrassed to help you when you fell." I swallow. "And too embarrassed to be your valentine. But I'm not now. Anyway, I figured even if I did apologize, you'd never forgive me."

I look over at Calli, and for a second she looks back. And I see all the hurt in her eyes (that I put there).

"And I gave you those flowers," I say, "because, well, I see you carry that laminated one around all the time, so I thought you might like a whole bunch of them."

She looks like she's going to cry. And I don't want her to. "Hey," I say, leaning forward. "Calli, I—" I look out at the parked cars again. "I like you."

Stuck

The Ferris wheel   stops

        with us at the top.
        I wish I could speak,
        tell Jinsong
        he's forgiven,
        that I like him, too,
        but my voice is stuck.
        So I rest my hand
        on top of his

        and breathe.

On Top of the World

Jinsong lifts our hands
above our heads.
"I like Calli!" he shouts.
"I like Calli June!"

And all the cool kids from school:

Duncan
Nyle
Ivy
Hazel
Gwyneth
Tilly
Grace

see and hear.

And in this moment,
though I am only on top of a
      Ferris wheel,
I feel as though I'm sitting
right on top of the world.
And my heart
shoots across the sky
like a star.

Knowing

On the drive home,
I glance out my window,
see the moon

so perfect
so beautiful

like Jinsong said,
showing off to the darkened world,
and suddenly,
I know—

know what I will paint for my self-portrait,
know what I will do when I am grown.

I won't be a florist like Mom.
I am smart.
I am strong.
I can do anything I set my mind to do.
And I set my mind to do this:

I am going to the moon.

The Moon

Contrary
to popular belief,
the moon is

not

made up of cheese.
It's made up of different
igneous rocks

and

hope   and
light   and
wonder.

Lying Awake

Calli's sleeping on the futon in the living room. *My* living room. And she's staying tomorrow night, too. If someone had told me yesterday how things would turn out today, I wouldn't have believed them.

I wonder what school will be like on Monday? Now that everyone knows I'm a "really nice guy"? Maybe everything will be fine. Maybe, just maybe . . . both sides *can* win.

Different

I waltz into D. Kahn's class
and everything is

                            different.

Besides the fact
that everyone is wearing
bright orange polyester suits,
there's a new feeling in the air.
It's light,
and joyful,
and brimming with adoration

                            for me.

Ivy and Hazel wave from across the room.
Their shoulder-length hair scrunches
higher, higher
until it is

                            short
                            short
                            short

as short as Jinsong's.

I ask them what's going on,
but as they open their mouths to answer,
the fire alarm goes off,
sounding so loud, like it's next to my

                                    head.

My eyes flutter open
and the classroom morphs
into Jinsong's living room,
his mother's cell phone
on the coffee table—

                                    ringing.

Sunday Picnic

I spread out the quilt,
while Jinsong and Chonglin
carry the pork-stuffed rolls.

Chonglin sits two inches from me,
watches me eat my roll.
"Do you have something on your eyeball?"
he asks, leaning close to my face.

I laugh.
"No, Chonglin. I'm winking.
It's a tic,
just something I do."
It feels strange talking about tics with someone
besides Mom or Dr. Flagner.

"Oh," he says, turning to his own roll.
He takes a huge bite.
"Does it bug people?"

Jinsong bops him on the head.
"Chonglin,
don't talk with your mouth full!"

Chonglin bites off another chunk.
"It's bugging me right now."
A piece of shredded pork
falls from his mouth to his plate.

"If people are bothered by her tics,"
Jinsong says,
"*they're* the ones who have a problem,
not Calli."

Jinsong winks at me and I wink back,
although my wink isn't on purpose.

Monday, Monday

Mrs. P'eng drops us off
on the way to her prenatal appointment.
Jinsong and I walk up to the school,
pass the flagpole,
open the front doors,

together.

I may be the only student wearing a polyester suit
with leg openings wider than my waist,
but suddenly I feel like I'm
dreaming again.

People are looking—smiling
at me.

At us.

Is this how it's going to be?
Like in my dream?
Is everyone going to like me now?

Small Blue Box

There's a small blue box
on my desk in homeroom.

Is it for me? It's got to be.

I want to open it.
But what if it's another prank?

I peer over my shoulder.

There's no sign of Duncan or Nyle
or strangely, Jinsong.

That's weird.

I wiggle the lid off the box.
Inside lies a heart-shaped locket.

> *Dearest Calli,*
> *I've always known we were destined*
> *to be forever friends.*

I crack it open, stare at the picture—

a teensy-weensy
Ivy Andrews.

A smile escapes my lips.
What. The. Heck?

Alone

Beatriz walks in,
freezes when she sees
the locket in my hands.
She yanks a book from her bag,
slams it onto her desk.

"So,
what kind of strange sounds
are you going to make today,
Cantaloupe?"
She says it loud enough for half the class to hear

but
no
one
laughs.

I pull out my own book,
wait for D. Kahn to get off the phone,
tell us what to do.

"Gonna flap your arms like a chicken?"
Beatriz continues.

"Or punch yourself in the face?"
She laughs.
But she laughs

alone.

Done

The tardy bell rings. I wish Duncan and Nyle would let me pass so I can get to class. But they won't until I answer their question: What was I doing at the top of the Ferris wheel, holding hands with Freak Girl?

I squint and shrug. "Why do you care?" I try to pass them again—we're already late—but Duncan shoves me back. "Has your brain gone cuckoo?" he asks.

I flinch. Is he kidding me? "No," I say. "I like her. Okay, guys? I like Freak Girl."

Nyle steps forward. "Ooh, and do you like those ugly clothes she wears, too?"

"Yeah," I say. "I do. And by the way, she only wears them to school so people won't notice her tics." As soon as I say it, I regret it. Shoot. I told.

Duncan and Nyle laugh, then imitate Calli—jerking their heads and puckering their lips.

"Stop it, okay?"

They keep going.

I curve my hands into fists. "I said, knock it off!"

They start croaking. I can't believe it. I am so done with these guys.

I wind my arm back, like I'm pitching a fastball, and hit them. Duncan first, Nyle next. Right on their chapped kissy lips.

I sprint up the hallway. Take a seat outside Principal Ellison's office. (She'll be calling me in there, anyway.)

Silly

I've always thought it sounded silly—
what Dr. Flagner said.

Because wouldn't
talking
about something
make it better understood?

At least much better than keeping
superquiet about it would?

I'm just a kid,
and he's the adult,
but here's what I think:

Dr. Flagner was   wrong.
Mom was   wrong.
Their advice was   wrong.

Trying to hide my Tourette's only
backfired,
             big time.

Between Classes

I hurry down
to Ms. Baumgartner's office.
Her door is open,
but she's not here.

There's a pad of Post-its
on her desk,
so I take one off,
pull out my lucky pen.

Ms. B.,

You were right!
Thank you.

Sincerely,
Calliope June

In P.E.

"Have you seen Jinsong?"   "Nope."
"Have you seen Jinsong?"   "Nope."
"Have you seen Jinsong?"   "Nope."

From Hero to Zero

Finally, Principal Ellison opens her door and ushers me inside. After a few minutes, Duncan and Nyle join me with their angry eyes and busted-up lips.

I study my shoelaces while Principal Ellison asks Duncan and Nyle a series of questions. She doesn't ask me anything. Just reminds me that Black Ridge has a zero tolerance policy. (Especially for the student body president.) Then she tells me to call my mother to come get me.

At Lunch

Ivy invites me to sit at her table
with her and Hazel and Gwyneth,
            but I'm not sure I should.
It's a little weird, they all of a sudden
want to be my friends.

But their table is
so
much
better
than the infected one by the garbage cans.
I'm lucky I haven't caught
hand, foot, and mouth disease yet.

I take the empty seat next to Hazel,
stab my straw into my juice box.

The interrogation begins,
only this time,
it's questions about Jinsong:

            "How long have you guys liked each other?"
            "Do you ever hang out after school?"

"What's his favorite color?"

"Have you kissed him yet?"

I happen to glance across the cafeteria
to where Beatriz has just gotten out of the lunch line.
She stares at me—
at the locket around my neck—
then shakes her head,
storms out of the cafeteria with her trayful of food.

Self-Portrait

On the canvas
that used to be white:

I swirl my brush around itself,
paint a golden circle

that rests in the hands of a
grinning girl

whose long hair billows behind her
like amber waves of grain.

On the canvas
that used to be white:

I paint gray for the ground,
black for the sky.

Mrs. Ainsley strolls by.
"Nice work!" she says. "The title?"

I trade my brush for pen, and then,
in large, loopy letters I write:

CALLIOPE JUNE
FLIES TO THE MOON

on the canvas
that used to be white.

I'm Next

Only twelve men
have walked on the moon,

have seen its craters
and mountains,
and rifts

have held its fine dust
between their gloves,
those shimmering specks of

gold
silver
brown.

In the Hall

Someone pokes me between the shoulders.
I spin around, hoping to see Jinsong,
but find Beatriz.

"I just want to warn you,"
she says with a fake smile.
"Ivy and her friends are only
pretending
they like you, but really, they don't."

"What are you talking about?" I ask.
And why should I believe her?

Beatriz smirks.
"That locket around your neck?
It's the same one Ivy gave me last year.
After a few weeks,
she made me give it back.
So, you know, enjoy it while it lasts.
'Cause when they're done,
Ivy and her friends

will
spit

you

out

like a chewed-up piece of bubble gum."

The Word

Monday is my mother's busiest day of the week. She sees her doctor, buys groceries, meets her friends for lunch, and takes Chonglin to his kung fu classes. So I have to wait until fifth period for her to pick me up. Normally I wouldn't mind being out of class all day, but whenever a student comes to the office window, they look at me, wide-eyed.

Yep. Duncan and Nyle have spread the word: Jinsong P'eng, Black Ridge student body president (and supposed friend to all), got suspended.

Where Is He?

When I look at Jinsong's empty chair in science,
Beatriz says, "He got suspended.
And it's all because of you."

I'm really getting sick of her,
lying and laughing all the time.

I'm sure Jinsong has
a good reason why
he had to leave school early.

Maybe he isn't feeling well?
Maybe his mom went into labor?

I Hate Toothbrushes

I would rather spend a year in Principal Ellison's office than three minutes in the car with my mother. It's the longest 180 seconds of my life. No questioning. No lecturing. No yelling. Just the hard face of a mother who is disappointed in her son.

For punishment, she gives me a marathon list of chores to be finished by the time I go back to school in three days. My two least-favorite chores are on the list: scrub the tub (with a toothbrush) and scrub the toilet (also with a toothbrush).

"And if you finish early," she says, "you can do them all over again."

Too bad *wash dirty clothes* isn't on the list. I'd really like to see Calli tonight.

Liked

The moment the final bell rings,
girls crowd all around me.
I get a million "good-byes"
      and hugs
      and high fives.
I grin and soak it all in.
Today is better than
Halloween
      or Christmas
           or my birthday.
I'm not going to let Beatriz
ruin this.
She's probably just jealous.

Happy Girl

I head toward home
humming,
strumming my fingers
along the chain-link fence.

I can't wait to show Jinsong
my necklace.
I hope he's not sick or hurt.
I slip my free hand into my pocket
over my "courage"
and sing—

"Happy is the girl
          with a poppy in her pocket.
Happy is the girl
          with a friend in her locket."

It isn't until I'm off the school grounds
that I notice—

a car,
following me.

Stranger

Oh no.
It's probably
a bad guy.
He's going
to snatch me up
in his fancy
black car,
drive me away to—
Nevada?
Yep.
The plates are from
Nevada.
I glance at the man
behind the wheel.
He's handsome.
And tall.
And smart-looking
in his black-rimmed
glasses.
He winks,
flashes me
a smile.
I knew it

I knew it
he's going to
get me.

Danger

I watch the scene in my head:

> *the car speeding away with me inside*
> *driving to the middle of the desert*
> *leaving me to rot in the boiling sun. . . .*

My heart pounds.
I'm too scared to run.
I press my back
against the fence
as the wheels creep

closer
closer.

I shrink to the sidewalk
like a
wilted poppy

waiting
waiting

to be picked.

Go Away

"Calliope?"
A voice says my name—
correctly.

> Go away. Leave me alone.

"Calliope, it's me."

I peek through my hands, see
black curls
red lips
thick eyebrows gathered with concern.

> "Mom?"

She crouches,
wraps her arms around me.
"Sweet Pea, I'm back!"

She's wearing old jeans,
but her face looks new—
all lit up
like it's bathed in a candle's glow.

I squeeze her neck.
"Who is that?"

"That's Reno, Sweet Pea.
He's your new stepdad!"

What? No.
Did she pull up to the convention center
and walk straight down the aisle?

No.
No.
No.
No.
No.

What was she thinking?

Exceptions

My father comes home early from work. Before he sets his bag on the couch, my mother explains to him what I did this morning.

"Good for you," my father says, undoing the knot in his tie.

I smile.

My mother does not smile. "Ru P'eng!" she says. "This is not a good thing."

"Sure it is. He stood up for his friend."

My mother throws the stack of tiny baby washcloths she just folded, and shakes her head. "No matter what, hitting somebody is wrong."

"No, not 'no matter what.' There are exceptions." He turns to me. "Jinsong, good job, Son."

My mother gets a look on her face—the same look she got when she tried the fiery-hot chicken wings from Domino's Pizza last month.

I lower my ball cap so it's over my eyebrows and back up toward the kitchen. I'm getting out of this conversation.

Somersaults

Reno,
who happens to not look anything like
Mom's usual type—
he's wearing clothes that
don't have any holes in them—
offers to drive me the rest of the way home
in his fancy black car.

"No thanks," I say,
and walk away.
I'm glad Mom doesn't stop me,
because maybe, just maybe,
I'll see Jinsong at the oak tree.

I shuffle along in a daze,
the contents of my stomach
doing somersaults.

"She's married,"
I whisper to the oak tree's new buds.
"How could she? She didn't even tell me."
I wonder if it was one of those
silly Vegas drive-through weddings?

That sounds like something she'd do.

Pots

Mrs. Sumner
has new pots on her porch.
They're small
and empty
and blue,
kind of like how I'm feeling,
but Mrs. Sumner waddles out,
fills each pot with

flowers
and soil
and love

purple pansies,
yellow and white daffodils,
and a fiery-red wonder
with a center as black as midnight.

Pain

I wait a while for Jinsong,
but the pain in my stomach gets so bad,
I speed-walk home.

By the time I reach the door to the apartment,
I've come to realize what Mom's marriage
really means—

> grab the keys
> pack the car
> hit the road
> don't look back

and I lose all my pizza from lunch.

Strike Three

The phone rings. It's for me, so my mother lets me take a break from dusting.

"Hello?"

There's a long pause before the person on the other end speaks.

"Hello, Jinsong. It's your student council adviser." Mr. Kahn's voice is soft and slow.

Crud. This can't be good.

"I've had a chance to speak with Principal Ellison regarding the incident this morning."

I chew my lip. Is it getting hotter in here?

Mr. Kahn continues. "We think it's in the best interest of the student body to appoint James McKinley to take over your responsibilities for the remainder of the school year."

The room spins. This can't be happening. But it is. And I should have expected it. After all, I signed the agreement on the first day—the agreement that had one sentence in bold type:

Behavioral problems may result in removal from Student Council.

I don't know what to say. I've let down the student body. I've let down Mr. Kahn. I've let down Jinsong P'eng.

I guess I was wrong. Both sides can't win. In fact, both sides lose. Three strikes, I'm out.

"I'm sorry," Mr. Kahn says.

Not as sorry as me.

Perfect

I lie on my *bed*,
stare at the ceiling in disbelief.
Mom sits by my side,
puts my hand in her lap.
She thought I'd be happy to hear the news.

"I think you'll like Las Vegas," she says.
"We'll live in a big new house," she says.
"Have money for more vintage dresses," she says.

blah
blah
blah

Just when things are finally perfect.
Just when everything gets good.
She has to go and ruin it—
take it all away from me,
just like
she took away
my amber waves of grain.

What About Tom?

I nuzzle my face deep into my pillow.
"What about Tom?
I thought things were good?
I thought everything was fine?"

Mom's words come gently,
like a floating feather
tapping my shoulder.
"Things *were* good. But Reno is best.
Reno is everything I've ever wanted."

Men

I had a dad. Once.
And there have

        always
        always

been boyfriends.

But I wish,
really wish,
it was just Mom and me.

      No husbands.
      No rings.
      No boyfriends.
      No flowers.
      No dates.
      No phone calls.
      No dinners.

And that's all I'm going to say
about that.

Uh-Oh

Right before dinner, Chonglin barges into the bathroom. "Calli's at the door for you!" I set down the toothbrush I'm scrubbing the toilet with and hurry into the living room.

"Hey!" I say when I see her. Then I notice she's twitching, crying, shaking. Crud. What happened?

"Where were you today?" Calli asks. It sounds more like an accusation than a question. "You weren't in homeroom, or science, or at the tree." I can barely understand her through her sobs.

"I know." I rub my chest. "I'm sorry. I got suspended."

She stops crying. "So, Beatriz was telling the truth? Oh my gosh—what happened?"

I pick a piece of lint off my T-shirt. "I—uh, I hit Duncan and Nyle. For being jerks."

Calli wipes her eyes. "Oh!"

"Yeah, it's been a pretty bad day."

Her voice gets all high-pitched. "Well, I had an amazing day." She starts crying all over again. (Girls. I don't think I'll ever understand them.) She sniffs. "That's what makes my mom's news so bad."

I shove my hands into my pockets. "What news?"

"We're moving to Vegas on Friday."

I try to act normal, but I feel like I just stuck my finger in a light socket. "What do you mean, you're moving to Vegas on Friday?"

Calli hugs herself. "My mom got married to some rich guy she just met. He's in our apartment right now."

Table for Three

Reno takes Mom and me
out for dinner,
to celebrate our new life as a family,
but I don't eat.
I'm scared I'll barf again.

During dessert Mom hands me
a small drawstring pouch.
"I got you something on my trip."

Mom and Reno both smile as I open the pouch,
pull out a jagged rock
with violet-colored clusters.

"It's an amethyst," Mom says,
but I already knew,
since it's my birthstone.
"There was a shop next to the convention center.
Thought you might like it for your collection."

Truth is,
I do like the rock,
and under different circumstances,
I might even love it,

might be thrilled Mom got it for me,
but I was really hoping the red sandstone
would be my last rock.
I wanted eleven and twelve
          the empty spaces
to stay that way.

I drop the amethyst into the pouch.
"Can we go home now, please?"

Moving Day

Mom says to come home
as quickly as possible after school.
It's moving day
and she'll have the Bug
     all packed up
     ready to go
when I get home.

I have to walk to school,
since Mom's busy jamming
last-minute stuff into the Bug.

Reno already went back to Las Vegas,
drove his fancy black car.
I'm so glad he's not riding with us.
I'll get to have Mom all to myself
before things change
forever,
or until Mom changes her mind.

Mom pokes her head out
to say good-bye.
"Smile, Sweet Pea, it's a gorgeous day!"

No thanks.
It might be sunny outside,
but I'm full of dark gray clouds
heavy with rain
that constantly drizzles
from my eyes.

Enough

I have my poppy with me
          for courage,
but it doesn't seem like
enough.
How can anything be
enough
on a day like today?

Then I remember the new blue pots.
The new blue pots
on Mrs. Sumner's front porch.

And I break into a run.

Pocketful of Poppies

Mrs. Sumner's inside her house,
watching TV.
I see it flashing through the window.

I crawl up the steps
on my hands and knees,
    almost sneeze,
but hold it in.

Quick as a kitten with a ball of yarn,
I grab the poppy stems,
yank them out,
stuff the whole bundle,
    soil and all,
into one of the back pockets
of my favorite denim shorts.

No more vintage clothes for me.

Back from Suspension

I zip through the commons as fast as I can. I don't care about the group of guys, whispering. Or the girls ignoring me. Or James McKinley, the new Black Ridge student body president. Or Duncan and Nyle and their we-just-smelled-something-funny faces.

I wonder how tryouts will go tomorrow? Will I be drafted to play with the Royals? Or will one of them? I've been working with Coach Todd every couple of weeks, but Duncan and Nyle have been going to the batting cages *a lot*.

However it pans out, the fact that we aren't friends anymore makes it easier to be going up against them.

One Good Thing

I'm about to take my seat
in language arts,
when a voice behind me says,
"You have a bunch of flowers
growing out of your butt."

I look over my shoulder
and down at my back pocket,
which is bulging with the poppies I stole
from Mrs. Sumner's front porch.

I whirl around,
look her right in the eyes.
"You know, Beatriz,
I'm supermad at my mom
for making me move,
again,
but if I can think of

one
good
thing

about leaving this school,

it's that I won't have to see *you* anymore."
I smirk as I sit in my chair,
spilling soil and poppies
everywhere.
"Oh"—I glance back—
"I'm glad you like my flowers."

Beatriz looks at her lap,
pulls out her binder.

Love Notes

On my desk I find:
love notes.
The first one reads:

I LOVE YOU.
TOO BAD YOU'RE MOVING,
WE COULD HAVE GONE OUT.

> *Nyle Jacques*

The second one reads:

Too bad you're moving.
I wanted to go out with you.
You are sooooo fine.
Hope you don't have a boyfriend,
because I really like you.

> *Love,*
> *Duncan Gray*

Not Today

I hear my "admirers"
behind me,
busting up,
waiting for me to cry or run.

Not today, boys.
I stand,

march
        march
                march

until we're
face   to   face.

Riiiiiip.
Riiiiiip.

Pieces flutter to the ground.
"Get a life."

Ivy's Table

I

      sit
      smile
      open my lunch.

They

      frown
      stand
      move over by the garbage cans.

What's their problem?
Did they see what I did
to Duncan and Nyle?

Maybe Beatriz was right?
Maybe Ivy and her friends are
done with me?

Ivy hasn't taken back the locket,
but it looks like she's taken back
her friendship.

Old Friends

After I get my food, I sit with Calli at Ivy's table. Or what used to be Ivy's table. For some reason, she and her friends are over by the garbage cans.

Calli says, "Wow. You got through the line fast."

"Beatriz let me cut in front of her." I take a bite from my taco.

"Oh. Yeah. I forgot." Calli sets down her sandwich. "You guys are . . . friends, right?"

"Not really. Well, sort of." I explain how Beatriz and I used to be friends. Best friends. Until her parents got divorced and her mother moved to Colorado. Said she couldn't handle three kids on her own, so she took the two younger ones and ditched Beatriz.

"And that's when she started being rude to everybody," I say. "Even me. At swimming lessons, Beatriz pulled the skin by her eyes and said, 'Look! I'm Jinsong!' and the whole class laughed and thought it was totally hilarious."

Calli smiles a sad smile. It makes me sad, too, thinking about it.

I whisper the next part so nobody else hears. "Last summer, when our families went camping together in Pine Valley, Beatriz told me how mad she is at her mother. But her mother isn't here, so she takes her anger out on everybody else." I pick all the tomatoes out of my taco and form them into a little hill on my plate. "But I really think that way down deep, like as deep as the Grand Canyon, Beatriz is still the friend I used to know."

Beatriz

Ditched
Deserted
Abandoned
Given up

Sure, Mom gives me bad advice,
and her dating decisions
ruin my life,
but at least she's in it.

At least I have a mom.

After the Last Bell

Locker cleaned,
I'm ready to go,
but my feet feel glued to the floor.

Across the hall,
Beatriz stands,
mouth turned down, books in her hands.

An idea hits—
knocks my breath,
like a zooming comet it slams my chest.

Digging in
my bag I find:
my lucky pen and a piece of paper.

I Write

Dear Beatriz,

This poppy isn't perfect,
in fact it's been
>   *neglected*
>   *wilted*
>   *discarded*
>   *pressed*
>   *and sat on every day for months.*

But, if you let it,
it will bring you courage:

courage to be nice again
courage to be the real Beatriz.

I hope you and Jinsong can hang out soon.

Your friend,
Calli June

P.S. If you want, I can e-mail a picture for the
locket as soon as I get to Las Vegas.

Beatriz's Locker

I wrap the gifts
with the note,
slip them through the widest slot,
then
listen, listen
hear them

d
r
o
p

hit the bottom with a *thud!*
—the same sound my heart just made.

Agreed

Jinsong meets me out front
by the flagpole,
instead of the old oak tree.
We walk slower than slow,
because as soon as we're home,
I'll get into the Bug and leave for good.

We reach 700 South,
the last turn before our apartments.
Jinsong rounds the corner,
but I keep walking straight.

     "Where're you going?" he asks.

I pause,
wipe my eyes with the back of my hand.
"You want to know something
about the moon?"

     "Sure."

"It's constantly moving
away from the Earth."

"No way."

"Way. And it'll keep on moving,
an inch and a half each year,
until maybe it's gone forever."

He walks over to me,
puts his face close to mine.
"But I don't want it to."

I swallow, whisper back,
"Me, neither."

We walk block after block
and we don't stop
until we reach the park.

Confessions

"I have a confession," Calli says as we sit beneath a tall tree. "Those poppies you gave me for Valentine's Day?"

"Yeah?"

"I put them in the garbage disposal."

My mouth twitches. "I have a confession, too. I watched you through the window."

We laugh.

"Sorry about that." She hugs her knees to her chest. "I thought you were being mean. Seeing those flowers made me think about how I don't fit in."

I bump her with my shoulder. "Of course you don't. That's what I like about you."

Cheese Puffs

Jinsong unzips his backpack,
pulls out a small bag
of cheese puffs.

They remind me of when
I first came to St. George,
how my heart felt
empty,
but now it's filled.

Will leaving
make it empty
again?

How to Share

As soon as Jinsong opens the bag,
I lean over to sneak a cheese puff,
but he quickly extends his arm,
keeping them out of my reach.

"Hey, if you're going to have
a baby at your house," I tell him,
"you're going to have to learn to share."

> "I already know how to share."
> He throws two cheese puffs into his mouth.
> "I live with Chonglin, remember?"

I stretch as far as I can,
snatch the bag from his hand.

> "Oh, my mother found out
> what she's having."

I squeal. "Well . . . ?"

> "Well what?"

"What is she having?"

Jinsong crunches another
cheese puff. "A baby."

I grab a fistful of grass,
throw it at his face.
"I mean, is it a girl or a boy?"

He wipes the grass away.
"Ohhh, that. It's a girl.
My mother wants to name her June,
because she'll be born June 1."

My breath catches in my throat.
June is the best month of all.

June

No sleepy drivers
coming home.
No snow.
No white.
No cold dark night.
No ice on roads,
just big green toads
and Popsicles,
and long hot days
spent running through sprinklers,
laughing.

Window Well

Calli won't stop talking about toads, so I am going to find her one. I scour the bushes, search beneath the pavilion, and turn over every large rock in the park. Finally, I jog across the street and check the window wells in front of some of the houses. Sure enough, I spot one wriggling beneath a pile of dead leaves. It's gray and green and a darn good jumper.

I jog back to Calli and set the toad in her lap. "Here you go. A nice, ugly toad for you."

She fake gasps and picks it up. "What? He's not ugly." She turns the toad around so it's facing her. "You're a handsome little fellow, aren't you?" Its sticky tongue darts from its mouth and hits Calli right below her nose. "Ew!" she yells, tossing the toad away from her. It hops toward the pavilion.

We fall over laughing and can't stop. My cheeks ache. My eyes are wet. Best feeling ever.

I sit up, dab my eyes with my shirt. The sight of Calli's short hair glowing in the sun hits me like a ball in the gut. Man. I'm going to miss her. "You remember that night during the moon festival?" I ask. "I wrote you a riddle and you couldn't guess?"

Calli chuckles. "Yes."

"Well, I feel bad you never got your prize."

She waves a hand in front of her face. "No biggie."

No biggie? No biggie? Um, huge biggie. I take a deep breath. "Well, I decided you can have it anyway."

"Oh!" She sits up. "Do you have it with you?"

I nod. Stick my hand into my pocket like I'm searching. "Close your eyes. No peeking." And while her eyes are closed, I do it—I kiss Calli June.

I Am

flitting

        floating

flying

up
up
up into the sky

singing

        sailing

soaring

higher
still
into the clouds

dancing

drifting

dreaming

all the way
up
to the moon

Sunshine and Me

I rest my head against the tree
the afternoon sunlight beams down on me
makes my eyes see sunset orange
behind their resting lids.

Jinsong asks when I want to go back.

But I'm not.
I'm not leaving at all.
Gonna live here forever
        and ever
        and ever

here in the park,
the sunshine
        and me.

"If you don't go back,"
Jinsong explains,
"I can't give you your gift."

My eyes flutter open,
see cinnamon again. "You got me another gift?"

He grabs my hands,
helps me stand.
"Yep. And I think you're going to
like it."

My Made-Up Proverb

Sometimes life is good. And sometimes it smashes you with a hammer.

Shot Down

Jinsong and I
walk up to the apartments,
      same as we always do,
as though we'd walked straight home,
as though school hadn't ended
three hours ago.

Mom gets out of the Bug.
When I see her expression—
a mix of worry and anger—
      I'm shot down,
down from my cotton candy clouds
and ground into the dirt.

"Where have you been?"

Packed

Mom wasn't joking when she said she'd be
   all packed up
   ready to go
   when I got home.

"I went for a walk," I tell her.
"I went for a walk with *him*."
I turn around, but Jinsong's gone.

   "Well, can you get in the car, please?
   We're running late."

Since when does she care
about running late?
"But I have to say bye to Jinsong."

   "You've spent quite a while
   saying bye to him already.
   Reno's expecting us. We need to go, now."

I back away,
from her,
from the Bug.

"NO!" I shout.
"Not without
saying good-bye!"

No Room

Mom's mouth hangs open like a dead fish,
but I don't feel bad for yelling.

Jinsong comes out of number fifteen
carrying something huge,
white.
He rushes down the stairs to the parking lot,
turns the huge, white thing around.

A bunny!

He hands me a stuffed bunny,
with big, brown eyes
and floppy ears as long as my arms.
"For you," he says.

for me
for me
for me

Mom takes one look at the bunny.
"Sweet Pea, that is NOT going to fit."

Wanna Bet?

"There's room for this bunny.
    This bunny.
    In there.
Right beneath my
    derrière."

Forget Me Not

I wish I had something
to give him,

like a bundle of forget-me-not
flowers. But I don't, so

I fetch my lucky pen
from my bag,

write my e-mail address
on the back of Jinsong's hand.

He frowns,
looks down at me.

"Bye," he says.
"Bye," I say.

I thank him for the bunny,
rip my eyes away

from cinnamon,
forever.

That Girl

Watching Calli leave is worse than getting suspended. Worse than getting a zit inside my nostrils. Worse than getting hit in the crotch by a baseball.

I don't get why people move away. It can't be fun to pack up their lives. Dump them in a brand-new place. I've lived in the same apartment for twelve years. (And I'm happy.)

I stare at the ink on the back of my hand. Trace the letters with my finger.

"Are you okay, hon?" my mother asks when I go back inside. I push past her huge belly and open arms and head straight for my bedroom. Okay? Of course I'm not okay.

I choose a random book from my shelf and open it, but I can't concentrate. And I don't feel like playing video games with Chonglin. Or helping my mother make dinner.

After pacing the hallway for a while, I finally sit at the computer and type in Calli's e-mail address.

Everything

Hush
lull
noiseless
still
except for the motor
running smooth
or the occasional sniffle
from a girl
who has just left behind

everything.

Wanderers

Ancient Greeks called the planets

     planetoi

because it means "wanderers,"
and because planets don't stay

       in
       one
       fixed
       place

they're constantly moving,
wandering between the stars,

like me.

On Our Way to Las Vegas

Thirty minutes into our drive,
I speak the first words
either of us has spoken
since we pulled away from the apartment.

"I have to go to the bathroom."

Mom takes the first exit in Mesquite, Nevada,
rolls to a stop at a gas station.
"Let's make it quick," she says,
as we both get out of the Bug.

I must be hurrying a little too much,
because the next thing I know—

slam!

I've shut

        my thumb

                in the door.

Evening Up

Mom rushes around,
opens the door,
      hugs me.
"I'll get some ice."

While she's gone
I try,
really try
with all of my might,
to
not
do
what I want to do—
what my brain
tells me to do.

But the feeling grows
      stronger
stronger
          stronger.

I have to make the pain
      even,

I have to make it
      symmetrical.

I open the door,
stick my *other* thumb,
      the uninjured one,
inside the frame.

Slam!

Subject: HEY

I know you just left (and probably won't read this e-mail for a while), but I'm really bored.

So, how are you? How's your new house? I have Little League tryouts tomorrow afternoon. I hope I make the Royals.

Write me back when you can.

Jinsong

Like This

Mom returns with a cupful of ice.
When she sees what I've done to my other thumb,
she swears,
hits the side of the Bug with her fist.
"Why?" she whispers.
"Why do you do things like this, Calliope?"

"I had to," I say, reeling from pain.

"No," she says.
"You didn't," she says.
"I don't get you," she says.

I shut the door in her face, tell her it's because
she's never tried.

Sick

The burning sun disappears behind the mesa,
just like my desire to please Mom.

I could say sorry
for what I did,
keep on keeping them inside—
      my feelings.
But what good has that ever done?

Mom joins me in the Bug,
sticks the key into the ignition.

I gather a deep breath in
and when I let it out,
a bunch of words come

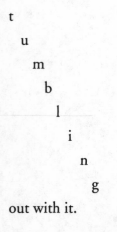

out with it.

"I'm sick of trying to hide my tics.
I'm sick of moving around all the time.
I'm sick of you switching boyfriends.
I'm sick of you taking things away:

> my hair
> my home
> my friends
> my life."

I straighten my back,
turn toward Mom.
"And I don't pull my hair anymore,
so you don't have to keep cutting it,
okay?

MY HAIR   is   MY HAIR.
I never wanted you to cut it!"

Married

Mom stares at the steering wheel,
crinkles her forehead.

      I raise my voice again.

"And how could you go off,
get married without telling me?
You could have at least called,
asked me if I was okay with it!
You could have waited until school was out,
or let me get to know him first.

      Reno could be a murderer!

And I have to go live with him?
Change MY whole life
because YOU like him?

Wait. Do you even like him, Mom?
Or do you just like his money?"
Mom bursts into tears,
which makes
me
burst into tears.

I Choose Toilet Paper

I'm watching Saturday-morning cartoons when my mother blurts out, "I need you to either massage my feet with peppermint oil or ride your bike down to Nolan's Supermarket and buy some toilet paper. Your choice."

I choose toilet paper.

On my way home from Nolan's Supermarket, I ride past a bright green house—a house I've seen a million times but never been to. Kenny Gunn is out front on his hands and knees, staring at the ground. I skid to a stop. "Uh, whatcha doing?"

Kenny's head snaps up. "Hey, Jinsong. I just got a new compound light microscope, so I'm collecting stuff to examine. You want to search with me?"

I've got nothing better to do, tryouts aren't until one o'clock, so I call my mother and ask if I can stay. She says yes, but not for too long. (Chonglin's going to need the toilet paper.)

Kenny and I examine pond water, dog hair, and spider mites. I learn a bunch of interesting things, but the best one of all is that Kenny Gunn really is the Nicest Kid in School.

Reno's House

Reno's house is

giant,
huge,
enormous,

so enormous, in fact, I wander around
for almost two days without seeing anyone,
which is

fine
with
me.

I have nothing left
to say to Mom.

Promise

Sunday evening,
Mom knocks on my door,
enters,
even though I didn't say she could.

"I'm sorry, Sweet Pea. Really, I am."
She walks across the room,
sits on my new bed—
      which is an actual bed,
      with box springs,
      and a real mattress,
      instead of just air.
"I know you don't like change," she says,
"and I've handed you a lot."

She reaches over to stroke my hair,
but I roll away,
squeeze my giant bunny,
stare out at the bright city lights.

"Can you forgive me?" she asks.

"Can you stop moving?" I ask.

I count all the way to twenty
before she answers me.

"I wish I could promise
that Reno will last.
I feel like he will. I hope that he will."

A tear slips from my eye,
rolls over my nose,
plops onto my pillow.

Understand

Mom may not understand me,
but I haven't exactly tried
to understand her, either.

And maybe I can't change
her
any more than
she
can change
me,

can't   change the fact she
can't   stand to be single,
can't   stand to not know

if the grass is greener someplace else,
just like she

can't   take away my tics,

or my need to eat my food
in a certain organized order.

I sit up,
throw my arms around Mom's neck.
"I hope that he will, too."

Updating My Rock Collection, Again

1. Granite from My Backyard
   (Spokane, Washington)
2. Greenish-Blue Thing I Found in the Street
   (Ritzville, Washington)
3. Cobblestone from an Old Riverbed
   (Walla Walla, Washington)
4. Basalt I Found on a Hike
   (Baker City, Oregon)
5. Piece of Pumice from My Teacher
   (Bend, Oregon)
6. Pebble from the Playground
   (Boise, Idaho)
7. Limestone from the Park
   (Pocatello, Idaho)
8. Lava Rock from Neighbor's Yard
   (Logan, Utah)
9. Salt Crystal from the Great Salt Lake
   (Salt Lake City, Utah)
10. Red Sandstone from an Ortho's Office
    (St. George, Utah)
11. *Amethyst from a Rock Shop*
    (Las Vegas, Nevada)
12. *Moon Rock ???*
    (The moon)

When I Am Grown

I'll go to college
       get my degree
sail up to the moon
       be happy
then settle down

stay
in
one
town

until my hair turns white as my name
and my skin is as wrinkled as raisins.

"Bea"

I stare at Calli's empty chair in science, thinking, maybe, if I focus hard enough, somehow she might appear.

She doesn't.

Mrs. Locke says a long word—*experimental*—and I can't help but think that if Calli were here, she'd repeat it a bunch of times. And if anybody messed with her, this time I'd do something to stop it.

"I'd like you to get into groups of two or three," Mrs. Locke says. The room becomes abuzz with students playing musical chairs.

I glance across the room at Kenny. He sees me and waves, so I grab my pencil and get up. On my way over I notice Beatriz, still in her chair. She's holding something that looks just like Calli's laminated poppy. Where'd she get it?

I slow down. "Hey, Bea."

She looks up and chuckles (but it comes out sounding more like a snort). "Bea?" She scrunches her nose. "You haven't called me that since—"

"—that time we went to the bounce houses?"

Her head bobs. "Uh-huh." She glances at the poppy, then back at me. "So, do you have a partner yet?"

I turn toward Kenny. "Yeah . . . but we could really use a smart girl in our group. You know Kenny Gunn, right?"

John Shepherd Middle School

I stand on the curb
at my eleventh new school,
wearing my *Gimme Some Space* tee
and a brand-new pair of jeans
that Reno bought for me.

Mom gets out of the Bug,
joins me on the curb.
She puts her arm around me
as we walk inside
together.

She's going to work with Reno now,
starting tomorrow morning,
creating floral arrangements for
all of the BIG weddings at
all of the BIG hotels.

I'm glad she came with me today,
because even though I've done this
ten times before,

I'm still scared.

Feeding Time

After she signs the papers,
Mom blows me a kiss
and I pretend to catch it,

put it on my cheek,
like always.

She walks one way
while I walk the other.
I make it seven steps before a long
beep sounds,
releasing hundreds of students
into the empty hall,
like feeding time at the zoo.

I press my back
against the wall so I

won't

      get

          trampled.

Lost

walk
stalk
      following the crowd

stop
study
      the map the office gave me

lockers
slam
      hallway getting empty

ask
boy
      acts like I'm invisible

wander
turn
      going round in circles

give
up
      trying not to cry

What to Do?

I lean against the cinder-block wall,
the waiting tears finally

f
a
l
l

make their way toward my neck.
Before I know it,
I'm playing scenes in my head:

> *me wandering the halls for hours*
> *wetting my pants because I can't find a bathroom*
> *the school nurse forcing me to wear clothes from the*
> *   lost and found*
> *hanging my underwear in the window to dry*
> *being forever known as the strange new girl*
> *who peed her pants on her first day here. . . .*

From: fortheloveofbaseball19@gmail.com

To: gimmesomespace27@gmail.com

Subject: HI

I don't know if you got my last e-mail or not. I sent it on Friday. I hope I have the right e-mail address. I'm sending this from my Exploring Technology class. So, how's your new school? What kind of classes do you have? Do you like your teachers? Sorry I'm asking so many questions.

Guess what? I'm the new pitcher for the Royals! Duncan and Nyle both got drafted to other teams. Well, I better go before Mrs. MacCabe sees.

I miss you.

Jinsong

Upside Down

A door shuts and footsteps behind me grow
closer, slower.

"Need some help?"
It sounds like a kid.

I rub my eyes, turn around,
hand the girl my map without a word.

"Oh," she says, "y'all must be new."
She squints at the map, turns it right side up.

I slap my head. Jeez.
I had it wrong this whole time.

"C'mon." She smiles. "I'll show you the way."
But before she does, she clasps her hands, says,

"OMG!
I love your shirt!"

We walk and walk and talk and talk,
like two friends conquering a corn maze.

Eventually we stop, although I wish we'd keep going.
I don't feel like facing a crowd.

Paige says she'll meet me back here in an hour,
help me find my classes all day.

Room 315

I knock on the door to room 315,
gently turn the knob,
push.

My heart pounds in my ears
and my face feels as red as the poppy
I left in Beatriz's locker.

I breathe in for a count of five,
let it out for a count of five.
I poke my head in,
scan the room for a teacher.

Oh, how I wish
that Jinsong were here.

With Me

"Hello," the teacher says,
"I'm glad you made it."

Yeah. Barely.
I cross the room, hand her my slip.
While she's reading it, I turn to the class,
suck in another breath,
blow it out.

"I'm Calliope Snow," I say,
"but you can call me Calli.
I just moved here from St. George, Utah."

I lick my lips. They're supersalty.

"I like comfy clothes,
I have a cool rock collection,
and someday,
I'll be the first woman to walk on the moon."

My throat makes a funny sound and
my arms jerk upward.

Tell them.

Tell them, Calliope.
Do it!

"I have a neurological disorder
called Tourette syndrome.
Maybe you've heard of it?
Sometimes I make faces or noises
that I don't mean to make.
So . . . if you happen to hear me croak like a frog,
just ignore me, okay?"

I laugh,
and twenty-nine students
laugh with me.

From: gimmesomespace27@gmail.com

To: fortheloveofbaseball19@gmail.com

Subject: JINSONG!!!!!!

My new school is gigantic,
so is Reno's house.

Congrats
on making the Royals!
That is superamazing.

Oh, good news: My mom said we
can visit St. George
the first weekend in June.
You'll probably have a baby sister
by then.

I miss you, too.

Love,
Calli

P.S. You want to know something
about the moon?

No matter where
you're standing on Earth,
it always looks the same.

AUTHOR'S NOTE

When I was a kid, I didn't know that I had Tourette syndrome, a neuropsychiatric disorder characterized by involuntary movements and sounds. I didn't even know that the list of strange things I did, such as twitching my face, taking exaggerated breaths, rolling my eyes, repeating words, or my least favorite of all . . . swallowing air (which made me sound like a frog) were called tics. I just thought I was weird. Really weird. In fact, I was the weirdest person I had ever met. And I was embarrassed by that. There were many times I pretended to sneeze so I could hide my facial tics behind my hands. Once, a friend of mine, who was genuinely concerned about my ticcing, asked me if I was okay, and I ran out of the room, crying, instead of explaining.

When I was finally diagnosed with Tourette syndrome as an adult, my neurologist looked at me and said, "If I were you, I wouldn't go around telling everybody that you have Tourette's." When I asked him, "Why not?" he answered, "Because it's a very misunderstood disorder. If people know, they'll treat you differently."

Days passed, and I thought a lot about what my doctor had

said. And I realized he was halfway right. Tourette syndrome *is* a very misunderstood disorder. But if I kept quiet about it, wouldn't that only contribute to it being misunderstood? So I decided to do something very scary. I shared my diagnosis with my family and friends, and even some strangers. And it felt wonderful. To let it all out. To feel a little more understood. Isn't that what every person wants? To feel a little more understood?

And so, my hope with writing this book is that readers will understand better than they did before what Tourette syndrome is, understand what it feels like to walk in the shoes of someone who does not have full control over some of the things they say and do, and understand that most people with Tourette syndrome have at least one other condition occurring alongside their tics that may or may not be obvious. For example, some of Calli's co-occurring conditions include trichotillomania (pulling out one's own hair), obsessive-compulsive disorder (eating food in a certain way, having intrusive thoughts, needing things to be even), and anxiety issues (worrying about everything). I still sometimes get embarrassed in public and try to hide my TS, but I'm learning to not be afraid. I'm learning that it's okay to be myself.

I'd also like to add that while Calli's tics and compulsions are based on my own experiences, each case of Tourette's—just like every person—is different. And different is good. Embrace what makes *you* different, and don't be afraid to show it to the world.

ACKNOWLEDGMENTS

Many thanks to . . .

My wonderful agent, Steven Chudney, for being willing to take a chance on me, and for his always helpful guidance and wisdom. My editors, Liz Szabla and Anna Roberto, for their patience and ability to know how to make a story blossom into something more beautiful. Designer Anna Booth for a breathtaking cover that is infinitely more gorgeous than anything I could have imagined. Production editor Starr Baer, copy editor Heather Hughes, and the rest of the Feiwel and Friends / Macmillan team for their time and talents.

Zhenyu Jin and MeiLien Lin for answering my questions about the Chinese Moon Festival. Linzee Hickman for answering my questions about baseball. The Tic Talk Facebook Group for helping me better understand the complex world of Tourette syndrome and for providing support since day one.

Joy McCullough Carranza—mentor, friend, and cheerleader—for loving this story enough to choose me and change my life forever. The 2014 Pitch Wars Facebook Group (TOT) for celebrating with me through the ups and carrying me through the downs. The

Swanky Seventeens MG/YA debut group for being my BFFs during this most awesome year in our lives.

Sarah Tregay, Rebecca Gomez, Myrna Foster, Stella Michel, Gayle C. Krause, Rachel Sarah, Peggy Jackson, Laura Shovan, Kelli Askeroth, Michele Askeroth, Breya Terry, Shari Green, Elizabeth Dimit, and Amanda Hill for reading early drafts and providing feedback.

My fifth-grade teacher, David Kahn, for introducing me to creative writing and for being the funnest teacher ever.

My mom for being my first and biggest fan. My dad for letting me use his typewriter at the kitchen table. And both of my parents for encouraging me to follow my dreams, even though the part about becoming a butter-sculptor never worked out.

My husband, Jeremiah, for not getting mad at me when I insisted on editing in the truck during the middle of a blizzard while we were hunting for a Christmas tree. Also for whipping up gourmet meals for the kids while I worked to figure out plot holes.

My amazing children (B, N, and K) for providing inspiration, for understanding what Mom's Writing Time means, and for welcoming Calli and Jinsong into our family as though they were real people.

And lastly, my Heavenly Father, who gives me all I have and is my closest friend in all I do.

Thank you for reading this Feiwel and Friends book.

The Friends who made

FORGET ME NOT

POSSIBLE ARE:

JEAN FEIWEL
publisher

LIZ SZABLA
editor in chief

RICH DEAS
senior creative director

ALEXEI ESIKOFF
senior managing editor

KIM WAYMER
production manager

HOLLY WEST
editor

ANNA ROBERTO
editor

CHRISTINE BARCELLONA
associate editor

EMILY SETTLE
administrative assistant

ANNA POON
editorial assistant

Follow us on Facebook or visit us online at mackids.com.

OUR BOOKS ARE FRIENDS FOR LIFE.